"What now?"

It was more of a rhetorical indication of the bad day I was having than an actual question. The bad day wasn't so much of a surprise as it was sheer probability. At the start of the month I had begun a science experiment in which I had traced the number of good days I had versus bad. Twenty days in, and I had only tracked three good days.

And now my side mirror showed a female police officer walking towards my driver side. My stomache was feeling uncomfortable, either a result of tense nerves or maybe just an after effect of the Taco Supreme I had just consumed.

My college graduation was merely two miles away but it may as well have been taking place in a galaxy far away. I took a moment to look around the car to make sure it wasn't messy in a damning way. I noticed a few Subway wrappers littered on the back seat. I had invested a decent amount of money in getting tighter abs, but it seemed the Jared diet only worked if you were starting it at two hundred pounds overweight. Overall, the interior of my car seemed a little less than embarassing.

I pulled down the window to see the officer scribbling something on a notepad.

"Do you know why I stopped you?" She asked.

"To fill your monthly quota?"

"You were twelve miles above the limit."

"Are you sure?"

"Yes."

"No I mean, are you really truly sure?"

She took off her glasses and looked me dead in the eye.

"Yes I am sure."

"Oh, ok."   My feeble attempt at confusing the officer had failed.

"License and registration."

" I usually don't speak, but I'm late to my graduation ceremony."

I gave a hopeful smile. What officer would give a guy a ticket on his graduation day? She walked back to her car to check my information as I looked at the clock again.

In truth, there was no great reason as to why I was late to graduation in the first place. I woke up that morning at the sound of the alarm clock, but instead of jumping in the shower I found myself watching the movie '500 Days of Summer'.

"Finally, an accurate portrayal of how love really is in the modern world." That's what I was telling myself as time wore on. My mind made a conscious effort to move, but my body felt disobedient and chose to linger without movement.

I still had a decent chance of making it to the free juice and cookies after the ceremony.

The officer returned a few seconds later with my license.

"I'm going to have to give you a speeding ticket."

"If you must."

"And I'm also going to have to ask you to step out of the car."

"Come again?"

"The Dale Bridge County police department has been looking for you. I'm going to have to place you under arrest."

Bye bye juice and cookies.

I was of italian heritage, with a mom who typically enough was a wonderful cook. What would she think about me getting arrested? Well, it woudn't be a thought so much as a blow to the head with her slipper, or a jab to the shoulder with a dustpan. Luckily I lived in Dale Bridge, which was a few hours away from where my parents stayed.

The ceromony must have been under way by now. I pictured the university principal calling my name.

"Anthony Hasher."

They would wait an appropriate minute or so for me to come to the stage before moving on. Meanwhile, I would probably be spending the day sharing a cell with a guy named Bubba Jo Jenkins.

"Can I ask what the warrant is for?"

"Code six thirteen."

"Ah yes, six thirteen. What does that mean?"

"Failure to return rental property."

I stepped out of my Honda Civic and scratched my chin.

"Is there any more specific information?"

"I'm going to have to take you in; they'll have more information at the jail."

Day twenty one was going to be the worst of them all.

"I'll try not to put these on too tight."

I grimaced as a pair of handcuffs were applied to my sweaty hands. These didn't feel like the fake pair I had played with as a boy. I had taken a wrong turn on the way to graduation and ended up instead on an episode of 'Cops'.

We left my car at the gas station and begin the journey towards jail. The back of the cop car looked very much like it did in movies. There was the metal fence separating the front and back, and the inability to open the back door from the inside.

"Thank you for being cooperative", the officer said as we drove away. She wasn't quite a looker. Maybe late 30s or so, appealing but clearly beyond my acceptable age range.

"I'm going to miss my graduation", I said to myself out loud.

"I never went to college", the officer said as she stared ahead.

"You didn't miss much", I answered and sat back in my seat.

It was twenty minutes of staring blankly ahead in the police cruiser before we pulled into the county jail. She helped me out of the car and we entered into a bleak looking building that had bare white walls and one singular room at the end of a long hallway. We walked to that room and stopped at the door.

"You have to stay in here until the magistrate is able to see you."

"Is this where you put the hardened criminals?"

"No. There is one other person in there; he's around your age."

She opened the door and I walked into the room. There were two chairs, a desk, and a television in the corner of the room. In one of the chairs sat a pale man who looked to be in his early twenties.

The officer advised me to take a seat and than she left and closed the door behind her. I looked at the man who seemingly had been sitting in silence before I arrived. He began staring at me as if we were old friends reuniting. I turned and stared at the wall on the opposite end of the room.

"How are you doing brother?" I heard him say. He had a booming voice, and the way he said brother reminded me of the Hulk Hogan interviews I used to watch as a child.

"I'm Don", he continued.

I turned back around.

"Anthony", I answered.

"First time in jail?"

"Outside of Monopoly? Yes."

"Always tough the first time. What did you do?"

"I failed to return rental property."

"That's tough brother"

"How about you?"

"I broke into somebody's house."

"Oh."

I was a little bit taken back at how casual he was about the whole thing. He had committed a far more serious crime than myself and clearly belonged in a different room. I remained quiet until he spoke again a moment later.

"I'm sure your wondering why I was trespassing."

"Not really. I'd rather just sit here in silence until the magistrate is ready for me."

"The police think I was breaking into his house in order to rob it. But, that was just a cover up."

"For what?" I asked as curiousity got the better of me.

"I was hunting."

The conversation had taken a turn for the weird.

"Hunting?"

His eyes widened and seemed to grow sharper.

"Yes. The man who lived there. I was hunting him."

I felt an urge suddenly to call for the officer but again I stayed silent.

"Well, he wasn't really a man actually."

I stood from the chair, which may have seemed a strange movement to him. I walked a few steps to the left and than leaned against the wall.

"Not a man?" I stammered nervously.

"That's right."

He stood from the chair also.

I than asked a question that for all intents and purposes I didn't really want to know the answer too.

"Than what was he?"

He opened his mouth but before he could speak the female officer walked in from a side door. She motioned for me to follow her.

"I guess I have to go."

"I'll see you soon", he said omniously as I passed.

I followed the officer out of the side door and in to another room. We were let in by a much older woman who allowed me to take a seat. My arresting officer handed some notes to the older women and than left.

"Mr. Hasher, how are you doing today?'

"I'm having some serous indigestion from a Taco Supreme. Everything else is peachy. Actually, I could do without the whole getting arrested part of the day. I did hear news about a possible Backstreet Boys reunion however, and I'll tell ya, that has me excited."

"Are you aware of why your here?"

"I would say I'm being punked, but I'm not quite a celebrity."

"You've been accused by a Mr. Harold Jamison. Do you know who that is?"

"No."

"He owns a video store, Movie Club."

Suddenly my misfortune became clear.

"You rented three movies from him a few months ago and never returned them."

"Wow. Who knew Mr. Holland's Opus could cause so much harm?"

"This crime is a misdemeanor with a maximum sentence of six months in jail."

"Can he really do this?"

"Yes."

"You know, Blockbuster doesn't even do late fees anymore."

"I'm going to let you post a free bail. But you have to appear in court in three weeks."

"That means I'll have to push back the meeting with my probation officer."

"You should take this a little bit more serious Mr. Hasher."

"I appreciate the advice."

Appreciated and disregarded at the same time. I signed a few pages of paperwork and they removed the cuffs and let me go. My arresting officer must have felt sorry for me because she gave me a ride back to my car even though it wasn't required.

I drove off from the gas station aimlessly. I had missed graduation, my lower back leg was itching, and my goatee had grown back uneven. Damn the world and it's unpredictable ways. There was nothing else to do but go home, which was my Uncle Lou's house.

I had original planned on getting a dorm, but a job was hard to come by and much of my college savings had gone into a new car. It seemed to make more monetary sense to live with Lou since he had so much free space at his house.

With college ending, I felt like I was on a train going nowhere. There was no set career waiting for me, and I had already forgotten nearly everything I had learned during the past four years. I knew I wouldn't move back in with my parents unless I was desperate. And even than, I would just join the circus as a rodeo clown and travel the country.

I settled on the couch and turned on the television. The news was on, and they were showing a picture of a girl who had a familiar face. Where have I seen her before? Had she rejected me in high school? No, those were typically brunettes.

It took a few seconds to place her. Becky Martin. She had gone to my high school, and was actually in my creative writing class during senior year.

Then I saw the headline beneath the picture.

"Whoa", I said out loud. I turned the volume up on the remote and listened closely.

"Just to repeat, twenty two year old Becky Martin has been found dead at Dale Bridge Park. There is one witness who says she saw a Black Honda Accord speed away from the scene."

"Everybody is driving a Honda Accord these days", I said to myself.

Uncle Lou came through the door a little while later. Lou was in his mid forties but already had a head full of gray hair. Even worse, he wore it curled completely to the left, unlike any hairstyle I had ever seen.

I stood from the couch to explain myself but he put his hands in the air.

"I'm not sure if I want to hear why every other kid was there except you."

"I was in jail. It was a big misunderstanding and I'm taking care of it so theirs no reason to tell my parents"

His expression didn't change. Typically, it was when his face showed the most resolve that he was truly angry.

"Why do these things always happen to you Anthony?"

"Gypsy curse? Horrible luck?"

"How many times do I have to tell you about luck?"

"It doesn't exist?"

"When you mess up, it's you messing up."

"But that's not what mom says."

"I love my sister, but she has never been right about all that pre-determination nonsense. Listen, God gave us all the free will to build our life. You either do it the right way, or you mess it up and blame it on bad luck."

My mom and my uncle were always arguing about the way life worked. She preached a consistent sermon of fate and destiny and advised me that all I had to do was go with the flow of life and I would end up wherever I was supposed to. Lou meanwhile thought that life was what you make of it. And than we had The Matrix telling me that to know the path is not to walk the path. Suffice to say, I was confused and a little bit on the fence about the whole thing.

I walked back to the couch and took a seat. I thought my uncle was done but he came and sat next to me.

"Are you tired?" I asked.

"It used to be worse. I can at least get up in the morning now, mostly thanks to ginseng and honey."

"I have to get me some of that. Hey, some girl from my school was murdered."

He looke d exasperated only for a moment.

"I wish I could say I'm surprised."

"What does that mean?"

"I mean that Dale Bridge has a few skeletons that nobody is proud of."

"Care to elaborate?"

"No. "

We watched television for a few minutes before he told me what was really on his mind.

"Anthony, I want you to see somebody."

I turned the volume down on the television.

"Who?"

"A fellow counselor of mine."

Lou was a therapist.

"Why?"

"He can help you."

I stood from the couch.

"Wait a minute. I admit to being goofy and possibly even eccentric, but crazy? In need of help?"

"Half of my clients are not crazy Anthony. They just are at a point in their life where they need to hear a different voice. Think about where you're at. College is over, things are changing, and you need guidance. And maybe you're starting to tune my advice out."

"I don't think I am."

"Maybe not purposefully, but I know how it works when you only have that one voice telling you how things are. Trust me, it will due you good. You're behavior the last year has not been healthy. I think your suffering from some kind of complex."

"What do you mean?"

"You need examples? Well let me count the ways. You were arrested and missed your graduation, you sleep in on the weekends, hell you could write a book about being lazy. Every day I see you mope around here without purpose. You have all the symptons of someone who is clinically depressed."

Depressed? I wanted to dispute his claim, but I realized he may have been speaking some form of the truth. Still, I wasn't quite ready to validate what he was saying.

"I know just the guy for you."

He took out a business card and a handed it to me.

"Take my advice this time and set up an appointment with him."

My uncle looked at me sternly.

The card read Mr. Ryan and had a phone number.

"I don't think its going to help, but I'll do it."

2

At night, I went to my best friend Robert's place, where he and his girlfriend Heather had invited me for a movie night. They showed me pictures from graduation, which I begrudgingly smiled at. It wasn't long before the Chinese food arrived.

I put the white carton of rice to the side and looked at the little fortune cookie. The fortunes usually lacked insight and personal relevance, but every once in a scarce while you could find a gem that actually fell under the category of genuine wisdom.

I looked up and saw Robert and Heather kissing between bites of rice.

Robert once was the constant party animal who lacked direction. He was always getting in trouble, either in class or with the law. But when Heather came into his life he became a touching story of redemption. Now everything seemed to go right for him. He was graduating with a degree in computer science and already had a profitable job lined up. I on the other hand was a broke English major with only a childhood dream of writing movies to rely on. All that I had to turn too for hope was the fortune cookie.

"There is no place like home", I read out loud.

At first sight I thought the fortune to be generic and without meaning. But the first sight isn't always the right one.

"Disgusting", Robert said.

"The food or the fortune?"

"Both."

"I guess the fortune is telling me to leave Dale Bridge and go home."

"Are you?"

"Naw I wouldn't be able to handle to the lectures. For now, this is home."

"It's also a place of murder."

"It takes more than one murder to become that."

"You guys haven't heard about Dale Bridge's shady past?"

"What do you mean?"

"Well, Dale Bridge may not be the safe slice of suburbia that we've come to know."

"It isn't?" Heather asked as she finished the rice.

I scratched my chin. "My uncle did say something about the town having skeletons in its closet."

"That kind of goes with the story I heard."

"Where did you hear it?"

"At some party."

"Tell us the story", Heather egged him on.

"Very well", Robert stated.

For added effect he took a moment to turn all the lights off in the apartment. We kept only the television on as Robert hit the mute button on the remote control.

"Let me guess", I motioned towards the window. "It all started with a dl ark and stormy night?"

"Don't be so cliché", Robert sat down in a chair next to the couch.

"A long time ago there was a teenager named Doug. He was kind of an outcast in school. You know the type, introverted and quietly wishing death upon the popular people. But there was one popular girl named Jessica who he had liked since Kindergarten."

"How did she feel about him?" Heather asked.

"Jessica liked him alright, but the problem was that she had a boyfriend."

"There is always a boyfriend." I said as I thought back to the social failure that was my high school career.

"Everybody in school seemed to know how Doug felt about her, including her boyfriend. Doug didn't care about him though; he still pursued the fair lady. He would go to her house at night, not actually inside, but he would just sit outside of her window and watch her sleep."

"That's so romantic", Heather said.

"And stalkerish", I offered. "I bet if Jessica woke up and saw Doug there she would have filed a restraining order."

Heather slapped me on the shoulder as Robert continued the story.

"Doug used to always approach her in the hallways and start up conversation. She took it innocently enough. But it was much more serious for him. He thought he was in love, that she was his soulmate."

Soulmate. The word would stay with me beyond Robert's story. It seemed too idealistic to be true.

"Despite his noble intentions, Doug started to make his love for her a little bit too obvious. He showered her with gifts and poems at every opportunity. The boyfriend finally one day got sick of it all. He ordered his gang to send him a message. A violent message."

"What a nice guy", Heather said.

"He waited for his boys to call him with an update, but they never did."

A strange chill filled the room, at least I thought so. I looked to see if anybody else was feeling it but nobody else stirred so I ignored it.

"They were dead?" I asked.

"Bingo. The bodies were found the next day, completely slaughtered. They found limbs; one of them had been ripped to shreds. The boyfriend couldn't figure it out. The only thing he could do was confront Doug about it."

"So than what happened to the boyfriend?" Heather asked eagerly.

"Please don't jump ahead of the storyteller. Alright, so the boyfriend went to an arranged meeting with Doug one night."

Robert froze again; it was like he had taken a class on how to tell a story.

"And he never came home." He said slowly.

"Now that's getting yourself out of the friend zone."

"They never found the boyfriend's body, but they assumed he was dead. The police suspected Doug, all the evidence and testimonies pointed to him. He knew he had to leave town before they arrested him. But he couldn't leave without Jessica."

"It's like Deniro says in Heat, you have to be able to leave the girl behind when the heat is coming."

"Would you leave me?" Heather asked Robert.

"Don't worry, I'd arrange for you to meet me later on in Fiji. So Doug went to Jessica's house one day, and she invited him in. And that's when Doug finally confessed how he felt."

I raised my hand. "Oh I know this story. Jessica said that she was flattered but that she saw him only as a friend."

"Actually, no."

"Oh sorry, that was actually an episode of Dawson's Creek. You know, high school for me was like Anthony's Creek, the flood years."

Robert sighed.

"She was hesitant. She liked him, even sort of cared about him, but her boyfriend had just died and this was all happening too quickly for her. So she told Doug that while she could love him one day, she needed a little time and space first. Doug told her he didn't have any time to wait. He needed to know her answer immediately. And he said that if she said yes, if she was willing to love him, then he could offer her something that no man would ever be able to offer her."

"So?" I said impatiently.

Robert leaned forward. "Immortality", he said simply.

To the common person this would have evoked confusion, but not to a major horror fan like myself.

"Are you saying what I think your saying?"

"Yes."

He leaned forward.

"Doug was a vampire." At the word vampire, Robert put the old Transylvanian accent into his voice.   "You know, creatures with fangs." Robert added.

As a more normal person, Heather seemed confused.

"Your story was realistic until now", she stated.

"Remember, I said this is a legend. If there was no Vampire, than the story I just described to you would have been as Anthony said, just an episode of Dawson's Creek."

"So what happened next?" I questioned.

"I'm glad you asked. He had confessed his true self. But, he didn't just tell her, he showed her. He brought out the fangs, and the ghoulish white skin, whatever it took to convince her. And when she was convinced, he started selling her on the idea of her becoming a vampiress. That's like a female vampire."

"So much for romantic", Heather said.

I noticed a plot hole in Robert's story. "Shouldn't she have been mad that he killed her boyfriend?"

"Yes, and she resisted at first, but he swore to her that he was innocent, that it had been self defense. And soon she was under his spell. She had always liked him, and now she knew that he was special. She agreed to become his vampire wife."

"Did they live happily ever after?"

"Well, that's when the police came in."

I laughed. "Say goodbye to any possible happy ending."

"They saw him leaning towards her neck, and they immediately thought he was trying to kill her. She saw them pull out their guns and screamed for them not to shoot. But it was too late."

The scene played out in my mind, vividly, as if I was there in person witnessing it.

"They shot him forty one times?" I asked.

Robert stopped and looked at me. "What?"

"Nevermind."

"He was dead a few minutes later. The girl was heart broken. She had lost her boyfriend and now Doug. She moved out of Dale Bridge the next day, never to be heard from again. I like to add my own epilogue to the story where the girl moves to a small town and becomes a waitress who than wins the lottery and.."

"So nothing ever came out about Doug being a vampire?"

"According to the story, no."

I sighed. It was a depressing conclusion.

"So the moral is that a guy should never confess his feelings to the girl he loves."

Heather stood from the couch. "I think this party where you heard the story probably had a lot of alcohol."

"But how could bullets have killed Doug if he was a vampire?"

Robert shook his head. "That's a quandary, I admit."

"And if the cops covered the whole thing up, how did some guy at a party know the story?"

"As I said, I can't say for sure how factual this story is."

"Hey, how did that girl Becky die again?"

Robert almost smiled than, as if his story was connected to everything.

"She had her throat ripped out."

"That sounds kind of vampirish."

"They are not real", Heather said. "I think I'm going go read a little and than sleep."

"You do look exhausted", I said.

"I've just been working lots of hours at the hospital", she said wearily.

"I don't know why", Robert said. "Even without any volunteer hours, you'll be accepted to any medical school you apply too."

She smiled uneasily.

"I'm just covering my bases. I'm sorry you missed graduation Anthony."

"There are way more important things in life than that. For example, what is the purpose of unsweetened ice tea? And can we pass some law that prevents people from ordering it?"

"At least you graduated", Heather said.

My grades in college were a bit of a sour subject for me. My professors had always gone out of their way to tell me that I had a certain amount of unrealized potential. I had never lived up to what they thought I could be. My parents had been saying the same thing since my conception.

"I did alright", I said.

"Anthony, you are a writer. You could have been an honors student."

"Writing is different. That's me being creative, not the same as studying. "

"Maybe you don't know how to study?"

"I don't think a Studying for Dummies book is required. I mean correct me if I'm wrong, but you simply go through the book and memorize what you read right?"

She nodded.

"Well, we can't all be Encyclopedia Brown."

"Robert had fun and managed to get good grades."

Robert put his hands in the air.

"Wait a sec honey. I'm a computer science major. There was no fun."

Heather's eyes lit up and I sensed one of her antidotes was on the horizon. "You know what I think? I think Anthony simply became absorbed in trying to be popular. You put so much focus in trying to be cool and getting girls that you stopped worrying about you're grades."

"No comment", Robert stated.

I waved my hand. "That is interesting, but flawed logic. "

"You disagree?"

"Sure, the idea of my grades slipping because I became obsessed with popularity is."

"Who said obsessed?"

"Very well, the notion that my grades slipped because of some need to be in with the 'in crowd' is flawed because most of the people who are with the 'in crowd' are actually good students themselves. These days, the trendy table is not the stupid table."

"Theirs a difference", she countered. "Some people have an innate coolness, to a point where it's effortless for them. For them studying hard isn't a distraction."

"So their coolness is natural, and I'm just a goofball?"

"I didn't say that."

"You said something pretty close to that."

And than she said something that she had said a few times before, only she was smart enough to word it differently every time.

"Why do you care if you're cool? Cool is just a subjective term used for people who go out a lot and wear designer clothes in an attempt to mask their own insecurities."

I rolled my eyes. "You're such a Topanga!"

"You sound like a late night infomercial for popularity."

"So if it isn't that, than what was it?"

What I said next was my best defense and also maybe the sad and bitter truth of it all.

"Maybe I'm just destined to be an underachiever."

I had never stated it out loud. It didn't feel so good.

3

"Hello Anthony, I'm Mr. Ryan, how are you doing today?"

"I'm good", I said quietly. He had a big office and two comfortable sofa style chairs in front of his desk. I took a seat and started to pick at my lips. It was an odd habit I had picked up as a boy. It's always the off-beat habits that we seem to hold onto.

Mr. Ryan looked far younger than Lou. He had dark brown hair, with lots of visible hair gel holding it up. He also was far more stylish, wearing a Calvin Kline designer suit. He tapped at a clipboard for a few moments before looking at me.

"So your uncle says that you just graduated college. How did that make you feel?"

"Educated?"

"But how did you feel about it ending?"

"Well, I guess I felt like Tim Robbins in Shawshank Redemption when he is standing in the rain after finally escaping prison."

"College was like prison for you?"

"That's overstating, perhaps like a country club prison that a celebrity goes too."

"So it wasn't that bad. Do you watch movies often?"

"Yes, all the time."

"Why is that?'

"It's a bit of an escape."

"Do you live vicariously through different characters?"

"For a while I wanted to be like Carrot Top. But I couldn't get the hairstyle quite right."   "What is your favorite movie of all time?"

"Rocky."

"I like that. I have the whole collection on Blu-Ray as a matter of fact."

"They are all good with the exception of number four. The Russian guy killing Apollo Creed in an exhibition fight was horrible writing."

He scribbled on his notepad a little bit more.

"I'm going to be honest about how your uncle described you. He said you were intelligent but misguided."

"I'd love to pat myself on the back but truthfully I just watch a lot of academies award nominated movies and pick up a decent vocabulary from them. If that makes me appear overly intelligent than I apologize for the misrepresentation."

"So you're saying you're not intelligent?"

"Correction, I'm saying that I'm not overly intelligent. I'm maybe the diet Pepsi of overally intelligent if that makes any sense. Actually intelligence itself is highly subjective."

"What kind of grades did you receive in college?"

"I had a two point five", I stated slowly.

He leaned back in his chair.

"I noticed you hesitated in telling me that. How does your grade point average make you feel?"

"There is no particular feeling that inhibits me about it actually."

"Are you sure you weren't embarrassed, or ashamed? It's alright to say it Anthony, the more things we can get out in the open the further we can progress."

I looked Mr. Ryan in the eyes. It was something I liked to do. I felt like

I could read most people like a comic strip. But, Mr. Ryan was doing a good job of appearing expressionless. Even his eyes were blank.

I took in a deep breath.

"Ok. It doesn't send a mountain of good feelings streaming through my body."

"You know you could have done better?"

"Much better"

"And what held you back?"

"I lacked the motivation to properly make use of free time in a productive fashion."

The words came pouring out of me like they had been locked away without oxygen.

Mr. Ryan just nodded.

"You know, many people are born with potential that never actually materializes during their life. Sometimes there are sociological reasons for it, but sometimes environment has no say in the matter. It's often just the individuals holding themselves back."

"But why do I do it?"

"Sometimes it's in the subconscious."

"Maybe we can get Christopher Nolan to help us?"

"I want you to ask yourself a question Anthony. What drives you to wake up in the morning?"

"I don't follow you."

"What gives you a sense of purpose?"?

"Easy. Cinnamon Toast Crunch."

I started to smile but noted the stern look on Mr. Ryan's face.

"Be serious Anthony."

I tensed up. "I guess I'm not sure."

He nodded, seemingly expecting that answer I had given.

"Have you heard of the man with no fate?"

"No, but I can guess the subtext."

"Tell me about the racing incident."

"So you know about that."

"A little bit. Were you into racing back than?"

"No. I never raced before that, and haven't since."

"What made you do it?"

"Blind ambition I suppose. My whole high school existence was like a book full of empty pages. It wasn't good, and it wasn't bad, it was just nothing. And if I had won that race, I would have been known for something. So I took a chance, and I failed."

"When you lose, don't lose the lesson."

"I didn't see much of a lesson."

"Maybe the race turned off your ambition. You were a good student in high school I assume?"

"Good enough to get into college."

"What are your immediate plans now that college is over?"

"I'm hoping to do an internship with the Men in Black."

"In the meantime?"

I took a deep breath.

"I've been applying to jobs around town. But so far nobodys hiring me."

"Any thought to graduate school?'

"I've considered Klown College. No, I don't think I could get in with my grade point average."

He nodded and stood from the couch.

"With the right recommendation you might."

I stood also.

"And that would come from you?"

"Only if I feel like you're heading in the right direction."

"How do I do that?"

"We have to take it one step at a time. I want you come back and see me in three days."

"I can do that."

I turned to leave.

"Anthony", he said.

"Yes?"

"Do you go out often?"

"To the video store."

"I think one thing that may help you is to meet some new people."

"I just spent four years doing that."

"Is there some special girl in your life?"

"No."

"You know, people with significant others tend to be happier about life."

"I had a girlfriend about a year ago."

"What happened?"

"She got bored."

"Did it hurt you emotionally?"

"Sure, but a little crack cocaine and I'm back on my feet."

Mr. Ryan was past smiling at any of my jokes.

"You haven't met anyone since?"

"No. The girls I aim for are usually out of my league"

"Some people let their standards be they're downfall. But the truth is that many of us aim for a masterpiece but settle for a compromise."

I walked towads the door.

"I think I get what your saying."

I pulled into the back parking lot of Pizza Village and sat parked for a moment. It seemed like a good way to make a little pocket cash until I found a better job. Still, nobody wants to deliver pizza fresh out of college.

I had first worked there when I was eighteen and desperate, and when I left during my sophomore year I never thought I'd have to come back. The hourly salary I received did not quite compensate for the way the manager treated me and the other employees. Sam Mryan was the unofficial pizza dictator of the East Coast.

You would figure the owner of this small pizza shop would be a kind, humbled man. What I got instead was a boss who must have thought he had opened up a string of Pizza Huts across the nation.

I walked into the backdoor to see my old boss standing there waiting, with an apron in his hand. By his looks, his career options appeared to be Pizza owner, or crime boss.

"Anthony, you're back! And you look exactly the same! Don't you know your suppose to fill out during college?"

"It's nice to see you again Sam."

"So I understand you want your old gig back?"

"Yes. I was also hoping we could talk a little bit about my salary. You see, when I left I was getting minimum wage. I was hoping maybe to get a little bit more this time around."

Sam began laughing, uncontrollably.

"Oh my, Mr. Smarty pants went to college and got a degree and now he thinks he should get paid more, is that it?"

"I think it's a reasonable request."

"Listen, writer boy, I know you got a degree in English, and I don't see how that makes you any more qualified to spin a pizza. But I'll tell you what. You put in a few good months of work, and I'll consider you for assistant manager, alright?"

I was not very good with negotiations. "Gee, thanks", I muttered.

He brought out my old uniform from the hall of shame and just like that I was a pizza boy again.

So this was where four years of education had gotten me.

My uncle may have been spot on when he estimated clinical depression.

I worked that very day, spinning pizzas and taking phone orders.

When you're down, it seems like the mind becomes the biggest tool. My best option was to simply change my mindset. Care free was the way to be. I began talking to myself internally, trying to convince myself with positive inner dialogue.

"I'm not sweating this job, I'm not sweating seeing a therapist, and I could care less about being alone. I'm doing just fine. I've braved the dangerous ledge, and had enough spirit to back away from it. I am the master of my own universe and I am what I choose to be!"

It was under this mindset that I received a phone call from Lou. He wanted me to do a little shopping for him on the way home from Pizza Village. It was a list including a bottle of Rolaids, a Spicy Chicken Sandwich from Wendy's, and an old Paul Newman movie named 'Cool Hand Luke'.

Some co-workers warned me not to go out because of the murder. I told them I'd be extra alert and careful. And just to ease their worries, I told them of a whiffle bat I had in my back seat.

I drove to Eddy's Video Buzz. I had never met or seen Eddy but I knew he was a real person since this was not a national chain but a townie owned video store. I was never going to go back to Movie Club again now that they had charged me.

It was a small but busy store, although I was by myself in the horror section. I often discussed movies on internet message boards. Eddy's had the recent remake of 'Black Christmas', but I was looking for the original, because it was known in cult circles as being the first slasher movie ever made. I had always thought that honor belonged to 'Halloween' but upon hearing differently on an internet message board; I had to check it out for myself.

As I looked around at various movie covers, I spotted an old couple staring at me with wondering eyes. They were whispering in each others ears about me. I immediately knew what they were thinking. A teenager in the horror section of a video store after a murder? Yes, they were considering me a possible suspect.

I saw an old movie I liked called 'Intruder', I went to reach for it but somebody else grabbed it first.

"Excuse me", the person said.

I turned to see a woman standing next to me holding 'Intruder' in her hand.

"No problem, it's a good movie."

"Oh, I haven't seen this one", she answered

It took a few moments for me to realize how attractive she was.

"Are you alright?" She asked.

It was her hair that was occupying the better part of my mind. Strands of long, straight hair. The color brown more fascinating than it ever had been. She wore an Oasis T-shirt and ripped blue jeans. I had been so overwhelmingly mesmerized by her that it had urged her to ask if I was alright. I told myself to be calm and cool even though my heart was doing jumping jacks.

The mystery woman had dark tan skin, but I couldn't quite place her ethnicity.

I noticed a silver bracelet across her wrist and thought it to be an easy compliment.

"That's quite a shiny bracelet."

She smiled, a nice easy going smile. And I was hopelessly dripping with infatuation.

"Thank you."

Mr. Ryan's advice played in my mind. This was my first chance to start anew. I decided to apply my new carefree attitude towards life to this very situation.

"Are you looking for a certain movie?" I asked.

For some reason I thought that learning her taste in movies would somehow reveal something key about her personality. I was already intrigued that she had been scanning the horror section.

"I'm in the mood for horror, or a romance perhaps?"

"Interview with a Vampire had horror and romance. I cried while watching it."

She hinted at a grin but not quite a laugh.

"Most men don't admit to crying."

"I don't cry to give up, I cry to move on."

"You're funny."

"Thanks, I took lessons. Playing the piano didn't seem as important. I don't mean to embarrass you and I'm sure you get this all the time but you're quite attractive."

"You're rather to the point aren't you?"

"I'm a realist. A realist who lives in a world of escapism if that makes sense."

"Not quite."

"Have you seen The Good Son?"

"No."

"It's with McCauley Culken. He took a break between Home Alone and Home Alone 2 in order to go psycho on Elijah Wood. It's a little bit light on the romance side and I don't know why I would be recommending it but it's the first movie that came to mind."

It's not always best to go with the first thing that comes to mind.

I looked beyond her and saw the old couple still whispering about me. Great, now they were thinking I was working on a new victim.

"Thank you for the suggestion."

"Now Leprechaun in the Hood, that was funny."

She nodded at my silly recommendation and turned to leave.

"So, do you go to school around here?"

She turned back around.

"I graduated college last semester."

"Same here."

"Do you often hit on girls at a video store?"

I was a little bit caught off guard by her directness.

"I usually don't see attractive women at the video store."

"So I'm the first?"

"Who says I'm trying to pick you up?"

"I'm sorry, I'm just being careful, with the murder and all its not that safe to talk to strangers anymore."

"We can solve that problem right now. I'm Anthony Hasher. There, we're no longer strangers right?"

"Are you a comedian?"

"Only in the shower. Now how do I know that you're not the killer?"

She looked at me incredulously.

"Do I look like a killer to you?"

"If I judged a book by its cover I would have thought Twilight was going to be an emo style mockery of vampires. Alright, well I guess in that case the cover was actually an accurate portrayal of the book."

"Do you read allot?"

"More so classic literature. I'm guessing you're a big movie girl?"

"Why do you say that?"

"This place here is only for people looking for older movies. If you wanted a new movie you would just go to Red Box where they only cost a dollar."

"But you need a credit or debit card for Red Box and I only have cash."

"I'm often wrong."

"No I'm kidding; of course I have a debit card. I just never had time for movies during school."

"Honors student?"

"Proudly."

"Were you cool in school?"

"I guess, why do you ask?"

"Oh, it's nothing."

"How was college for you?"

"I had time for movies."

"Did you maintain a healthy grade point average?"

"I wouldn't say healthy, but not quite cancer-ridden either."

"That's good, I guess."

"Do I really look like a potential killer to you?"

She took a moment to look me over. Lou once told me that when you first meet a women she decides right than and there if she wants to be in your company. He said that the whole idea of progressively winning a girl over was merely a fictional lie perpetuated by television and movies. As she looked me up and down, I couldn't disagree with old Lou.

But I didn't mind her checking me out because I didn't consider myself to be a bad looking guy. At least my mom had always told me I was cute. If you must know specifics, I was of average height, with a decent amount of muscle in my right arm, and nice Fonzie like hair. But I wasn't quite dressed to impress on this night as I had a black T-shirt and jean shorts on. Shorts, damnit, that was going to hurt me since I had noticeably weak calves.

She picked up American Beauty and we ended up at the register a moment later. I had Cool Hand Luke in my hands as I watched her pay for the movie and than turn to me.

"Have you seen Serendipity?" She asked as she moved towards the exit.

"Yes, I like John Cusack. But I'd rather not wait seven years to see you again."

"It's just that I'm leaving town in a few weeks. It was nice meeting you though."

She stood there for a moment. I guess she wanted me to bow out nicely.

"Enjoy the movie", I said. And than, as quick as she had come, she was gone.

I walked back to the register.

The cashier rang up the movie and I paid him three dollars.

She walked back into the store forty five seconds later.

"I'm Vanessa. Do you have jumper cables?"

I was not bitter that her initial decision had been to never see me again. That's what happens with most encounters in life. You make small talk and than leave. It's almost awkward for it to go beyond that stage unless you work with that person, have a history with that person, or go to school with that person. It's the main reason why I don't understand how people in the adult world meet new people and eventually get married. It seems on the surface that there are too many compromises that have to be made by each person for a relationship to work.

I couldn't help but think that fate was toying with me again.

Still, when something good happens, you try not to question it in the moment. I was well aware that Vanessa and I were only beginning a relationship through sheer circumstance. Either way, I had a little bit more time to hang out with her and change her mind about not wanting to see me again.

I actually didn't have any jumper cables but I offered to give a ride to the nearest gas station. My blue Honda Civic at that point would have qualified for 'Pimp my Ride', but she didn't seem to mind as she sat on the passenger seat and stared ahead.

"What did you study in school?" I asked.

"I was an art major."

"I didn't have a financial advisor so I majored in English."

"It was such a melting pot of different people and different cultures. I'll never have that again."

"Well we can always go to the international house of pancakes. So where are you from?"

She laid back and closed her eyes for a moment.

"My parents are from the Philippines. There wasn't much opportunity there for them so they came to America."

"Did you grow up in Dale Bridge?"

She shook her head.

"I was raised in North Carolina."

"They have great basketball players there."

I don't know why I considered that to be relevant.

"My parents are divorced; I came here to stay with my mom for a little while."

"Well, it's nice to meet you Vanessa. I didn't get your last name."

"Salisbury."

We drove for the next thirty seconds in complete silence. When I looked her she was staring straight ahead. It was when I stared ahead that I saw her out of the corner of my eye looking at me. It was quick, but it was a look that I would describe as both suspicious and curious. And she still managed to be completely exquisite as she did it. Than she asked a question of her own.

"And what is your story?"

"My story? Well I live here with my uncle."

"I wouldn't call that a story."

"Some nights we make pasta instead of chicken."

"Thrilling. I hope I'm not being too presumptive, but you should try living a little bit."

"That's a haste assumption isn't it? I am living, breathing air and everything."

"Are you sure you're not just existing? Everybody on the earth exists, but not everybody lives."

"Well that's pretty philosophical."

"Thanks."

I thought about it as we pulled into the gas station.

"Should I go jump out of a plane or something?"

"Don't be silly."

I parked in the front and accompanied her inside. I held the door open as she walked through.

"Sorry, I'm silly by nature."

"Your one of those nice guys huh?"

I didn't quite know how to take that. The only thing nice guys were famous for were finishing last.

"How are you folks doing tonight?"

The cashier at the gas station was an old, gray haired witch. At least, that was my first impression of him. I was waiting for him to put a curse on us when he instead handed us jumper cables in a box and smiled.

"Thank you." Vanessa said.

"Hey hold on a second, I'm going to grab a Red Bull."

"Those things are bad for you."

"I can't really 'live' and worry about my health at the same time now can I?"

"Fair enough. Grab me a Yoo-hoo please."

I walked to the back of the store where the cold drinks were. I was getting a bit drowsy and I still needed to go to both Wendy's and CVS to complete my mission for Uncle Lou.

After I grabbed the drinks, I noticed a strange man standing next to the protein bars. He wore a brown flannel shirt, blue jeans, and a cowboy hat. It was an odd clothing choice, as it made him look like a rougher Tim McGraw. But he was strange in my mind only because he was stuffing protein bars in his left jeans pocket. What do you do when somebody is shoplifting right in front of you? A heroic stand up guy either tries to stop him or goes and tells the cashier about it.

But I just went about my business. Hey, it was only protein bars. I didn't need the hassle of a criminal having some type of vendetta against me. That's how it always started in movies at least. You rat somebody out, they do a bid in jail, and than they come out rehabilitated with nothing but revenge on their mind.

Vanessa was in front of the cashier purchasing a pack of gum as I approached. She waited by the door as I paid for the drinks a moment later.

"You have a great night", the cashier said as the man in the Cowboy hat soon stood to the left of me. He had a water bottle in his left hand, a jeans pocket stuffed with protein bars, and in his right hand he had a giant gun.

"Nobody move!"

Vanessa stood against the door and looked at the robber.

"Are you serious?" She asked.

The question seemed to annoy the robber.

"You damn right, now shut your trap"! He replied.

The cashier looked worried as he opened up the register and started to take cash out. I stood blankly with the Red Bull in my hands. I wondered if I should try to take some type of action against the criminal. But those thoughts of heroism passed quickly as fear started to take over.

"Hurry up with the money"! He shouted.

Vanessa grabbed my hand. I turned to see her pointing her head to the left of the register where there was a box of Slim Jims sitting. I looked back at her in confusion. Did she really want me to try to attack the robber with a beefy Slim Jim?

"Now you two, give me all the money you have in your wallets!"

This guy was going for the jugular. I took out my wallet and emptied out a pathetic seven dollars. Vanessa was a little better with fourteen. He laughed at us cruelly and stuffed the cash in his other pocket.

I nudged Vanessa. "So does this happen to you often?"

"Hey, at least you're living a little bit now."

All the principles of a successful robbery seemed to be in place as the robber had the cash in his pocket and an open path to freedom. But as he walked to the exit, something else caught his eye.

"What's that?" He said as he looked at Vanessa.

She looked to me and then back at him. "What's what?" She asked innocently.

"What is that on your wrist?"

She looked down and than up. We both knew what the robber was referring too.

"It's a bracelet."

The bracelet had an undeniable charm to it. It didn't appear expensive and it wasn't gold, but there was something magnetic about it. It sparkled, elegant in a sense.

"Give it to me", the man in the Cowboy hat demanded.

Vanessa looked like the wind had been taken out of her at the mere suggestion. She locked a firm grip on her wrist.

"You can't have this."

That soft voice now filled with contempt.

"Your loyalty is valiant, but women I assure you if you refuse to hand it over I'll blow that pretty head of yours in pieces."

He didn't have the most sophisticated vocabulary but Vanessa got the point as she took the bracelet off her wrist and held it in her hand.

"You don't know what this means to me."

"No, but I will know what it means to me when I get it appraised!"

It occurred to me that a robbery was just a robbery if it went smoothly, but when something went wrong it had the potential to turn into something worse. With that in mind, I was hoping that Vanessa was going give up and hand over the bracelet.

"Listen you Larry the Cable Guy wannabe, you can't have this", she said boldly.

It didn't sound like she was wavering.

I wondered what was so special about the bracelet.

"Lady, I'm going to count to three. And if you don't give me the bracelet, I'm going to shoot you dead right here and now."

I looked at Vanessa and saw that she had a scary type of resolve in her eyes, as if she was willing to die for the cause. She took hold of my left hand

and I thought it might be a fitting time for me to chime in.

"Hey Vanessa, maybe you should consider reconsidering considering our situation?"

"What did you just say?"

"I don't know."

'One", the robber said calmly.

Vanessa grabbed my hand tighter. Was she expecting me to save the day? My only shot at being a hero was getting bitten by a radioactive spider and than being given a moment to take a nap. Than when I woke up I could sling a web at the robber!

Damn false hopes. We were goners!

I didn't know what to do. I kept waiting for her to stop his counting but she held the bracelet in her other hand just as tight as she was holding my hand.

"Two", he said as the gun made a clicking noise. I knew that noise very well. In movies, it was the noise a gun made when somebody was getting ready to use it.

I closed my eyes for a moment and pictured to myself what was about to happen. He was about to shoot Vanessa, and all for what, a bracelet?? What could I do to stop it?

I opened my eyes.

"Wait!!" I said.

Both the Robber and Vanessa looked at me.

"What did you say boy?"

"Just wait a second. She'll give you the bracelet."

Vanessa let go of my hand and looked at me.

"What are you doing?" She asked.

"Saving your life? He's about to shoot you!"

"You don't know that for sure."

"He just said he would. And than he'll probably shoot me and the cashier since we're witnesses"

He put the gun up to her forehead.

"Let me tell you something Lady. I have no problem killing you. I have killed before and history does tend to repeat itself. Back when I was a kid I..."

"Hey, we get the point", I said as the killer turned his gun to me.

"I mean, with your permission sir we'd rather not hear about your childhood."

He turned the gun back to Vanessa.

"Your boyfriend is right; I will kill everybody here if you don't have over that bracelet."

"He's not my boyfriend!"

All things considered, that comment stung me a little bit more than it should have.

"It's do or die time honey."

Vanessa looked at the bracelet desperately. There was nothing else left for her to do. She handed it to the robber.

"Thanks honey", he said as he made his way around her towards the door.

I looked behind him through the clear doors and heard a police siren. Than we all saw a police car pull up to the front. Perfect timing.

The robber turned to the cashier. "You hit the silent alarm didn't you?"

The cashier put his hands up and backed away as the gunmen pointed at him.

"You forsaken scudgoat! Why did you do that?"

With his attention turned to the cashier, I thought it was a great time for Vanessa and me to make a run for it. I motioned to her to run but she was still grieving over her bracelet.

The cop sat in his car talking on his radio, I guess calling for backup. I was waiting for him to come in and save us, but he wasn't making a move.

The robber than grabbed Vanessa and held the gun to her head.

"Sorry sugar, I thought the bracelet would be it, but it looks like I'm going to need a hostage to get out of here."

"Let go of me!" Vanessa cried. I was waiting for my own survival instincts to take over, but I started to believe that maybe I didn't have any.

I looked outside at the cop who still didn't look like he was going to be making a move any time soon. Where was an action hero when you needed one?

When I looked back at Vanessa I saw her slowly fiddling with something in her pocket. The gunmen was yelling something at the cashier as Vanessa pulled out the pack of gum that she had bought. I immediately sensed what her plan was. She was going to jab him in the eye with the gum. I shook my head at her to let her know that I thought it was a plan doomed for failure. But, she was a stubborn girl.

"We'll just wait until I can make a list of demands", the robber said. I didn't think much of his intelligence by this point. He could have easily escaped through the back door if he had any common sense. But in our situation, he who had the gun had the power.

"You smell awfully good", the Robber said as his nose traced along Vanessa's neck. My blood was boiling now as I started to think of what I could do to get him from away from her.

"I hate you", Vanessa whispered to the robber who didn't seem to take offense. He actually seemed quite taken with her.

"You know darling, there is a real thin line between love and hate." He smiled a toothless grin that didn't say much about his hygiene.

He kissed Vanessa on the cheek.

With all her might she smacked the pack of gum across his face. It hit him mostly in the nose but the end of it caught him in the left eye.

"You devil"! He screamed as he let go of her and she fell to the ground.

"That's it for you bitch!"

I threw myself at him, hitting him in the shoulder and taking him to the ground. Bravery is not really a character trait so much as something that we're sometimes forced into.

When I was a kid, a female doctor had told me that I would grow to six feet tall and make a great football player one day. Sadly, that prediction had not come close to being true. I thought back to high school when I had tried out for the football team and had been cut on the third day of tryouts. They said I hadn't tackled hard enough.

The gun slipped out of his hand which was the best thing I could have hoped for. I had control for about four seconds before reality struck. I was barely a man and this was a much stronger criminal. He pushed me off easily and than threw a right hook that caught me square in the jaw. I quickly discovered the downside of heroism. It didn't feel too good when the criminals beat you up. As I laid there in pain, I saw him pull a huge silver knife out of his pocket.

"I'm going to cut you up real good", he gave me a crooked smile as he raised the knife in the air. I said my last wishes, which were for a quick and painless death. Although, I anticipated a high amount of agony in getting stabbed. I had almost accepted it when I heard a loud thud.

It wasn't loud enough to be a gunshot. I opened my eyes and saw

Vanessa standing above me with the gun in her hand. The robber was on the ground next to me unconscious.

"Are you ok?" Her voice eased my pain.

I shrugged, trying to sound manly but my voice came out high pitched. "I guess so."

She offered her hand, and as I got up we both looked down at the robber.

"You really nailed him."

"He was going to stab you."

She reached down to the robber and grabbed her bracelet.

I looked at her and said "I'm glad you're alright."

What happened next truly caught me off guard. You see, she had saved my life, so there was no reason for her to suddenly be attracted to me because of my heroics. I had acted like a mild mannered citizen, not a superhero. But, crazily enough, she began to lean in a little bit. As I was told by some girl named Natalie in the eighth grade, when a girl leans in it means she wants to kiss you.

Where my heroism had never showed, my natural male instinct made me lean in with my lips parted.

We touched lips. I thought mine to be a little bit dry, but kissers can not be choosers. It lasted about six seconds and than she slowly pulled back.

We stood there, maybe both of us not knowing what to say.

The police officer came in just than.

"Are you folks hurt?"

"I think I stubbed my toe." I complained weakly.

Pretty soon we were back at the video store standing near Vanessa's car which now had a loud and roaring engine.

After she kissed me, I was feeling a little bit more at ease.

"Do you want to get a cup of coffee?" I asked her.

She stepped into her car and closed the door. She than rolled the window down.

"I'm driving this time."

I made my way into the car.

"If you don't mind me asking, what is so special about the bracelet?"

She held it tight for a moment before looking up.

"It was my grandmothers."

We ended up at a Waffle House down the street. It was famous for its bugs and for the waitress always telling you're her life story. I ordered a cup of coffee, and Vanessa ordered a chocolate chip waffle and hash browns. She poured both Maple and Butter Pecan syrup all over her plate before digging in.

"Hungry are we?"

She chewed the food thoroughly.

"I love breakfast foods." She said with a big smile.

I was actually contemplating ordering a Salisbury steak."

"Very funny."

"So a Red Bull is bad for me but for you waffles and hash browns are ok?"

"Hey, life is short."

"I suppose so."

"Your concern is sweet."

"Well if it makes you happy then indulge away."

"I'm sorry about being sour back at the video store."

"Hey, love means never having to say you're sorry. Love Story, 1971, Eric Segal. "

She didn't quite know how to react to my verbal works cited.

"So where are all your friends tonight?" She asked.

"Probably with his girlfriend."

"I had lots of friends back in North Carolina."

"I learned a while ago that you can't rely on friends."

"So you're a loner."

"What do you mean?"

"Do you want a hug?" She asked.

"Where is this coming from?"

"I'm not sure. You just seem kind of depressed, you know?"

"Do I?"

"Yes, when I first saw you in the video store, I just sensed you were unhappy."

I cursed myself for making it obvious. I had tried to radiate a good sense of humor and self confidence to spare. But she had come away with the impression that I was a depressed loner. The best route seemed to be changing the subject.

"So I guess the petty thieves are coming out of the woodwork since the cops are busy investigating the murder."

"Yeah I can' belive a girl died."

"She went to my school."

"That's crazy."

"I didn't know her well or anything."

I sipped my coffee steadily. Hazelnut, tasty but needed more cream.

"So you're leaving town?" I asked.

"I'm going to culinary school in California."

"I reckon you'll be seeing more cable guys named Larry down there."

"Oh no please don't say that."

"So what type of music do you like?"

"My taste is pretty eclectic, but my all time favorite is Pat Benetar."

I searched my mind but no images came forward.

"Who is that?"

"You have never heard the song We Belong by Pat Benetar?"

"I guess not."

"It's the greatest. So where do you work at?"

Buzzkill. I thought to myself, this is where I'm going to come of as a loser.

"I'm a pizza delivery boy by day."

"And at night?"

"A pizza delivery boy at night also."

She looked at her cell phone.

"I think I better go", she said.

Wow, was she materialistic enough to lose interest solely because of my horrible occupation?

"My mom doesn't know where I'm at, she'll be worried."

That at least sounded reasonable.

"I was actually just renting a movie for my uncle."

"Well", she said, 'We should both go."

I didn't know exactly what I wanted to say so I just stopped thinking and let the words flow out.

"Can I have your number?"

"No."

She said it without hesitation. She wanted nothing to do with me.

"Just kidding.   Haha, to see the look on your face."

"That is pretty cruel. So I can have your number than?"

"No."

"I guess I'm confused."

"You can give me your number. I don't give out mine normally because my mom monitors everything including my cell phone."

I put my number in her phone.

"Now, remember, you can only call me from the hours of 1AM to 12AM, ok?"

"Got it"

She turned to leave, and I touched her on the arm.

"Yes?"

"Thanks for saving my life."

I turned to leave but she called my name.

"Anthony, I have to tell you something. I just don't want you to get the wrong idea. I should have told you before we came here."

"What is it?"

"I have a boyfriend."

Misery not only enjoys company, it prefers that company to come back frequently.

"Hey, no biggie. Friends can talk over waffles right? And, they can kiss too."

"I'm sorry."

I put my hand on my heart and tapped it.

"You crush me."

"I don't mean to."

"And yet the effect is the same."

"Hey, what are you doing tomorrow night?"

"I'm not sure, why?"

"There is this carnival in the Wal-Mart parking lot. Do you want to go?"

"Just you and me?"

"And my boyfriend. It will be fun."

Fun in the same way that a route canal is, I thought to myself.

"What's the fellow's name?"

She looked a little bit uncomfortable at telling me her boyfriend's name.

"Ricky Winston."

The guy who I had raced during high school.

It figured as much.

"AHHHHHHHHHHHHHHHHHHHHHHHHHHHHHHHHHHH."

My eyes opened suddenly, painfully adjusting to the normal settings of my bedroom. I mumbled incoherent nonsense to myself for a few seconds before looking at the clock. Four thirty in the morning. Had that been a human scream I had heard?

"What the hell?" I said out loud. I sat up and than got out of bed.

Where was it coming from? I walked towards my window and slowly opened the curtains to check it out.

I didn't detect anything unusual outside. The front lawn was deserted, and still needed to be mowed. The mailbox was still slightly crooked. I was about to close the curtains when I noticed some movement in the bushes across the street at Mr. Drunkenmiller's house.

It's probably a cat, I thought to myself as I closed the curtains and jumped back into bed. The noise had interrupted a wonderful dream in which I had been sailing abroad, the captain of my own ship. They called me Captain Coconut, the bravest Captain on the exotic Island of Riches. We had been hunting for a treasure that had been lost for thousands of years when that awful noise had brought me off the ship and right back to reality.

As I prepared to try to find my way back to the ship, the bushes came back to my mind. The bushes moving, and somebody screaming, what could that be?

My worries were heightened because of the murder

I had to know that nobody was in trouble.

I threw on my shirt and jeans and stumbled down the stairs as quietly as possible. I looked in the closet for a flashlight but couldn't find one. Uncle Lou was asleep and I didn't want to wake him. I would have to go at it alone.

It was a far cry from the Island of Riches as I stepped onto my front porch and looked across the street at the bushes which were now perfectly still. I felt like Jamie Lee Curtis in Halloween when she's walking towards her friend's house, not knowing that Michael Myers has murdered her friend and is waiting there for her.

My steps were slow and cautious. I kept stopping to look around me. The lights were off in all of the houses I could see, which meant that everybody was sleeping. I was nearing the bushes now, my thought being that it had just been a cat that caused all that commotion. It was a reasonable assumption since there were always stray cats on this street wondering about, looking for a home.

Mr. Drunkemiller's bushes sat in a row with four big bushes with a decently sized level of space in between them. I stood in front of them, peering into a sea of nothingness. Should I really go investigating without a flashlight? My vast knowledge of horror movies told me this was a bad idea, sin worthy almost. Still, my conscience took over my better judgment. I just needed to confirm my thoughts that everything was fine.

I gently touched the bush softly with my finger at first, cautious as if it was something fresh from a hot oven. My intention wasn't courageous; I was just trying to alert anybody or anything in there that I was there to investigate. It was silly, but it was too late at night and the situation was too precarious for me not to be just a little bit paranoid.

Silence and bleakness possessed the night, a full moon serving as the backdrop for what appeared to be little more than my imagination playing tricks on me. It easily could have just been the wind that had moved the bushes. There was a light breeze. Yeah, that had to be it.

I put myself right in-between the first and second bush, and looked around. The bushes had a few sharp branches, and they were large enough to fit a litter of cats. That was still my best guess. What it didn't explain was the fact that I had heard screams, not the kind of shrieks you hear from a cat, but a human scream. Could my imagination conspire with my ears to make me hear something crazy?

An odor seemed to catch my attention for a moment. It was in passing, disappearing before I could decipher it. I took a step out of the first two bushes. Everything had been clear, now I needed to look between the third and fourth bush. My hands were starting to get cold, and my eyes were aching for sleep. Still, everything had to be checked out. I took a step into the third bush, placing my left foot in the space been the third and final bush. There were no sounds, no odors, nothing but silence.

It was empty, just leaves and dirt, and I began to relax. My nerves had surely built up a little bit, but my suspicions of the bushes having nothing to write home about were starting to come to fruition. People think they see weird things all the time, and it usually ends up being nothing. This was another case of the mind playing games with the eyes. I felt the call of my ship in the distance. A glass of chocolate milk before heading back to bed sounded swell.

I turned from the third bush and looked at the fourth. The only place I hadn't looked had been behind the fourth bush. What were the odds of the last bush having anything different than the other bushes? I could already taste the chocolate milk and even a toaster strudel sounded kind of tasty right than. Still, I had never seen Sherlock Holmes close the case before finishing the investigation. I took a step towards the fourth bush.

It was only when I was completely behind the fourth bush that I felt something brush up against my left shoe. My leg seemed to be caught up in something. Damn tree branch, I though to myself as I looked down. What I saw was not a tree branch, it was something blurry at first, than it became clear. Through the spaces between the leaves, I could see the hints of human flesh. Wait, that couldn't be right.

I crouched down and looked closer. I fell back in shock.

To the left of the final bush, under a few leaves and a branch, was a body.

No tricks with the eyes, it was clearly a body.

I expected myself to scream, as people always do in movies when they find a body. Instead, I just stood there quietly, without any idea of how to proceed.

I guessed it was a man going by the body's build. It was too dark to make out his face though. He had a blue t-shirt on with dress pants, an odd combination.

I figured I would call 911 and than hide in my closet.

I stood up and turned to run across the street.

The hand that belonged to the body suddenly grabbed my leg.

This time I screamed.

My arm wouldn't stop shaking as the hand finally let go of my leg and the body started to move all over the place. It was like a man having been frozen for years and than suddenly thawing out. The body had looked dead, but now he was more alive than me.

"Hey", he said as he started to get up, grabbing leaves out his hair. "Are you alone?'

I was still in shock, but managed to answer back "yes."

"Can I get some help here?" He asked as he reached out his hand. I pulled him out of the bushes.

He had long dark hair, like a member of an 80's rock band. He was still throwing leaves off his clothes as he stopped and looked at me.

"Hey brother, you're Anthony Hasher right?'

"How do you know my name??"

"I'm Don Crammers."

That body had a name, and it was familiar.

"I met you in jail right?"

"That's it, how are you doing brother?"

I was tired, spooked, and had dirt and leaves on my clothes. Still, I was relieved that he was alright.

"I'm fine. Do you lie in the bushes often?"

He looked around for a moment and than looked at me for a few seconds.

"Oh yeah. I was just taking a killer nap. "

"I did see something on the discovery channel once about a bush being a comfortable sleeping place. But I think that episode was about worms."

"I was having a bodacious dream until you woke me up."

"Well, I was sleeping too but I heard a scream and then saw the bushes move so here I am."

He looked over at the bushes. "I guess I move around a lot when I sleep."

"And the scream?"

He shook his head. "I didn't hear any screams."

I tried to read his eyes to see if he was lying but his expression didn't give anything away.

"You shouldn't be out here; it's not safe."

"Yeah I know."

I scratched my head. "So you're telling me that everything is alright?"

"Sure thing brother."

I hesitated as I sensed that he was giving me an incomplete truth. But hey, none of this was my business. I figured, why get involved?

"Ok than. I'm going to get back to my ship, I mean sleep. I guess you're going to stay out here?"

"Yes, that's right."

"Well, bless you and have a good night."

I started to walk away but he called my name. I turned around and came back.

"Listen brother, I'm dying to tell somebody."

He looked anxious as he spoke. I really didn't want to hear what he was about to tell me.

"This has something to do with what you told me in Jail? About hunting?"

"Yes. You remember I said I was hunting them?"

"And they would be who?"

He got real quiet for a moment, like he was about to reveal the mother of all revelations.

'The Vampires. Well, in this case just one."

I stood motionless. Robert's story flashed in my mind. And Becky Martin.

"Have you heard of Vampires?" He asked.

"Yes, of course."

"Do you believe they exist?"

"I'm open-minded."

"What if I told you they were real?"

"You have proof? Have you actually successfully hunted one?"

"No, and to be honest I don't enjoy sleeping in the bushes. I'm out here because I'm hiding."

"I thought you were hunting them?"

"That was than, this is now."

"What changed?"

He took a deep breath.

"I was in over my head. The vampire is far more than I can handle."

"He knows about you?"

"I don't think I should tell you any more. He might hear us."

I looked around.

"I don't see anybody else out here."

"He's out there, trust me. They have amazing hearing abilities."

"Listen, you're welcome to come in the house if you want. You can sleep on the couch."

He shook his head.

"I don't want you to be involved brother. You may already be in danger. I think your safe but if he is around sees you out here with me, it could be big trouble".

"But if they're out here, won't they come after you?"

He nodded and took a little metal cross out of his pocket and held it by his chest.

"They can't hurt me as long as I have this. You should maybe think about getting one."

"Do they have them at Wal-Mart?"

"This is no joke Anthony."

"Why don't you tell the police?" I asked

"Do you think they would believe me? I mean, do you even believe me?"

"I can believe there may be something weird going on in Dale Bridge."

His eyes got wide with excitement. I believe he was shocked to find a potential believer. He was probably expecting an extreme amount of skepticism on my part.

"Listen, I'm going to go back to sleep". I said.

"Fair enough. Hey, thanks for checking on me brother."

I waved my hand. "Sure, I mean I guess you can never be too careful right?"

7

"Are you married?" I asked Mr. Ryan who took in a deep breath.

"Seventeen years."

"Happily?"

"Yes."

"Any kids?"

He nodded and held up one finger.

"My son and I are not as close as I would like. He's off doing his own thing."

"Oh. I don't know if it's a similar situation, but even though i love my parents, sometimes the pressure they put on me drives me away."

He nodded and thought to himself for a few seconds.

"I try not to put pressure on my son. But this generation, your generation, is so individually minded. It's hard to get through."

"I guess I never really looked at the situation from the parent's perspective."

"Why did you ask if I was married?"

"I met a girl last night. I thought maybe it was relevant."

"That was quick."

"Yeah, but let me ask you something. Should a guy ever pursue a girl who has a boyfriend?"

"Is the boyfriend a large man?'

"Well, he's no slouch. I have a history with him and not a good one either."

"Are you scared of him?"

"No. Truth is, who he is makes me want her even more. Is that crazy?"

"It seems like you've really fallen for this girl."

"Yeah, I mean fallen may not even be a strong enough word."

"This is big time progress."

"I definitely got out of bed a little bit easier this morning."

"Does she have good teeth?"

"What do you ask?"

"It's this thing a professor taught me once. If she has good teeth than it's a good sign that she's a winner."

"I'll look for that."

"Well I'm happy for you; you're on the right track."

"I guess. But what about the boyfriend?"

"Anytime you put your heart out there its a risk. But it may be a risk you have to take."

I was lost in my own world, completely consumed by Vanessa. That was maybe my first big mistake. If I had stayed away from her, the events that followed would never have taken place. I would still just be a pizza boy instead of....well we'll get to that soon enough.

As it was, I was on a high that night as I waited on my porch for Vanessa to pick me up. I had agreed to go to the carnival even though it meant hanging out with Ricky Winston.

She pulled up a moment later. Her car of choice was a Blue Acura RSX. I hopped in noticed how much cleaner her car was than mine.

"So where is Ricky?"

"He'll meet us there. He had to pick up his friends."

"How thoughtful of him."

"So how are you feeling?"

"About the carnival or life in general?"

"Let's start with the carnival."

"Great, who doesn't enjoy carnivals?"

"Do you?"

"Well no, not particularly."

"And life?

"The less said the better"

"Your positivity is inspiring. Hey I thought we'd hang out at my house for a while until Ricky is ready."

"Sounds good."

She smiled and I noted that she had a perfect set of teeth.

The grass was neatly cut as we walked up the driveway of Vanessa's gigantic brick house.

It was a very upscale residence, with a Persian rug and portraits from famous artists posted up against the wall. I took my shoes off without her asking and didn't even dare to breathe on anything in fear of possibly tainting it.

She offered me a seat on her sofa.

"What does your mom do anyways?"

"She's an accountant."

"Very nice."

"Do you want to watch a little bit of American Beauty?"

"Sure."

Kevin Spacey had won an academy award, but I thought the rest of the movie was a little overrated.

She stopped the movie about ten minutes in when she got a text message from somebody.

"Ricky?"

"David."

"A friend?"

"Yes, from school."

"Do you keep in touch with many people from school?"

"I have their numbers, sure."

I suddenly thought of the movie 'There is something about Mary'. Could it be that I was just one of many potential suitors for her?

"Does Ricky know about these guys?"

"Yes."

"He doesn't mind?"

"I'm not cheating on him."

I guessed she didn't consider kissing me to be an act of cheating.

"I suppose not." I was about to say more but my voice seemed to trail off.

"He trusts me."

"And you don't think any of these guys are into you?"

"Maybe."

"And you're fine with that?"

"I can't control that. If a guy likes me he should make it known at the start before we become friends."

"Well, as a gentleman I carry no expectations, except maybe a better movie next time."

"That's all you want?"

"Before I ask for more I think we should go on a date first."

"Cute."

"Is that a yes to a date or a no?"

"I have a boyfriend."

"I have room in my backseat for him."

"You're crazy."

"Why? It only seems fair that he should get to tag along."

"I shouldn't have kissed you."

"We can pretend that I initiated it."

"So what do you do for fun?" She said, changing the subject.

"I play board games."

"Do you have siblings?"

"I'm an only child."

"So you play board games with yourself?"

"Um, yeah."

She stood from the couch. "Do you want some pie?"

"Sure, what kind?"

"Pecan, I just baked it."

"I don't think I've ever tried that."

Her eyes lit up.

"What do you people eat around here?"

"Apple pie?"

"C'mon, you have to try a slice."

She showed me to the kitchen where surely enough there was a brown pie sitting on the counter. I took a bite and was amazed at how good it was.

"Wow, this is really delicious. You made this yourself?"

She smiled proudly. "I want to be a chef."

"You don't see too many female chefs."

"That's very sexist of you to say."

"I mean on television. They don't have many shows with a female chef."

"Well, I want to change that."

"And I want to eat at your restaurant some day."

She pierced my heart with her smile.

"And what are your plans?"

"I don't know yet."

"Why not?"

"The twenties are supposed to be a time for exploration and adventure. I don't want to get tied down to a serious life just yet. I guess I'm kind of undeclared about the future."

"Well time isn't slowing down."

"Thanks mom."

I realized that around her I felt like I was at peace with life. But how attached did I want to get to a girl who was leaving and had a boyfriend? A good woman was like quicksand. And I already felt myself sinking deep.

After the pie, she made us both a cup of hot chocolate.

"This is really good", I said after a few sips.

"What would you expect from a future all-star chef?"

"I'd love to see you bake a cake."

"If you're nice, we may some day get to that point."

We finished the hot chocolate and stood in the kitchen. Ricky called a moment later.

The carnival ended up being about ten minutes away from her house. We arrived at nine thirty to a packed crowd; seemingly every line had a ride. Vanessa wanted some cotton candy, so I bought her some, although it hit me that there was no reason for me to be performing boyfriend activities for her since she actually in fact had a boyfriend.

Ricky showed up around than with an entourage of two, his buddies Sam and David, who seemed like relatively nice guys. Although Ricky looked the same physically, I knew that things had changed for him. He wasn't an athlete any more, having traded in his running shoes for an insurance license.

After the race, Ricky came to Dale Bridge just as I had. He was looking forward to a free ride through college on a full scholarship, but he hurt his knee during freshman year and all hopes of him being a future track star went out of the window. He was tough; he tried to finish the race even after twisting his knee. But, it only made his knee worse.

It had to be tough, going from being a highly recruited athlete to suddenly attending a local community college and having to start over. But having Vanessa as his girlfriend was not a bad consolation size.

"What's up Anthony?' Ricky said upon seeing me. He of course hugged Jamie first, than kissed her, and took a moment to take in the sights and sounds of the carnival, but after that, he looked over and noticed me standing to the side. Although we ended up in the same area, we hadn't spoken since the race. This time he seemed to remember me.

"Ricky Winston, it's been a while. How have you been?

"Real good man. I'm finally getting my speed back. I beat some chumps on the hill last week."

I looked in his eyes and tried to detect some new level of insecurity that he hadn't had in high school. To his credit, he seemed as confident as ever. I had long matured past the idea of hating him. When I thought back to high school I now saw him as being too full of himself to be modest, but at least not an overblown egomaniac.

But, just like before, we had been thrust into the roles of competitors. Although he didn't know it yet.

He held his arm around Vanessa, who seemed comfortable in his grasp.

"So you guys ready to hit some rides?" He exclaimed.

They all slapped hands and we were off to buy the tickets.

As it turned out, the rides at this carnival were about as exciting as standing in the line at the DMV. We struggled through them before Ricky suggested we go on the big Ferris wheel. How convenient, the guy with the girl suggests the Ferris wheel. They sat in a two seater, cuddled up, while I sat with a sixty year old woman named Edna. Edna had just saved money on her car insurance by switching to GEICO and she wanted to tell me all about it.

We soon spotted a little stand where you could throw a dart at a board and win a teddy bear for your girlfriend. Ricky, super boyfriend, was quick to grab a dart and dedicate his impending victory to Vanessa. But he would soon realize that running a fifty yard dash was not the same as throwing a dart. He missed entirely and than scratched his chin as if it was a fluke. I did what any guy in the pursuit of a woman would do.

"Hey, can I try?"

Ricky threw me a suspicious look.

"If you think you can do better, sure."

I threw Vanessa a hearty smile as I grabbed a dart and focused in.

Be the man, I told myself.

A voice answered back from somewhere deep inside, "you are incapable!" It's funny; my inner voice sounded an awful lot like my dad's voice.

I aimed the dart in front of my face.

I then flicked my wrist, and closed my eyes.

"Wow!"

It was Vanessa's voice, the exact one I had been waiting to hear.

I opened my eyes, and saw that my dart had landed right in the middle.

She hugged me then. It was just a friendly squeeze, nothing intimate as her boyfriend was standing right to the left of us.

Ricky looked cautiously ecstatic. He had to be a bit angry that I had upstaged him. But in a show of good sportsmanship, he slapped my hand and congratulated me.

I looked at Vanessa and basked in the moment of her smiling face.

Either by coincidence, or in an act of tactful strategy, Ricky started to get romantic. It started with a hug and a kiss, and than he was whispering things in her ear and making her laugh. That's when I began feeling a bit uncomfortable. Who was I to meddle in their relationship?

We were walking when I saw a tent that had a big sign that said "Have Your Future Predicted with Madame Craziel."

I decided to take a little break from the happy couple.

"Excuse me guys, I'll catch up with you in a few minutes."

"So, you want to know the future eh?"

I looked at Madame Craziel and slowly nodded my head.

"I did pay six dollars."

"Sorry sugar, we used to be four dollars, but you know how the economy is."

The strange woman than took a moment to slip into character.

"But......." she paused before continuing."Are you....ready for what the future may hold?"

A single bead of sweat raced down my forehead as I calmly nodded my head. I looked around me and saw plush red towels plastered all over the small tent. We were sitting at a small table that held a crystal ball, a deck of cards, and a tall glass of water with a lemon twist.

"I don't know if I really believe in all of this psychic stuff. I mean the only point of reference I have is Miss Cleo and she went out of business for being fraudulent."

"Give me your palm and I will ease all your worries."

"Alright."

Madame Craziel. Short, stubby women with Chia pet hair and a cat named Pebbles. You have to question the credibility of a psychic having a last name that sounds so much like crazy.

She grabbed my hand and held it steady. She closed her eyes and a moment later started bobbing her head as if she was Will Ferrell in Night of the Roxbury. I didn't quite know what to think as she started to raise my hand up and down.

"Shinnnnnnnnnnndddddddiiiizzzzzlllllle", she cried out suddenly. I was half expecting the room to start shaking. She than placed my hand on the crystal ball, which was a little bit below room temperature.

And then, it was over. She opened her eyes slowly and let go of my hand. I sat back in my seat and awaited her conclusion.

"Very, very interesting", she said as she wiped her forehead.

"What did you see?"

She held a finger up as she turned to her black cat Pebbles and took a moment to feed her what looked like a small bowl of crunch berries. She turned back to me.

"I have good news and very bad news."

"What is the bad news?"

She took a dramatic deep breathe.

"You are going to die."

My mind flashed to a patient at a hospital being told the very same news and breaking down and crying. But, this was not that serious. I was after all sitting in a tent with a woman named Craziel and a cat named Pebbles.

"You mean, like in seventy years right?"

"You are going to die SOON!!"

She emphasized soon and I gulped. My knees didn't go weak or anything, but you have to admit, this was not the kind of psychic experience that warmed the heart.

"Is that the worst news you've ever given anybody?"

"Yes."

She was either very serious or a really well trained actress.

"So how do I die?"

" I see a huge cloud of trouble entering your life."

"Perhaps I'll buy an umbrella."

"Remember how I said there was good news also?"

"I come back from the dead?"

"No, but you do experience true love."

"Are you sure this is not a story that you give to every one hundredth customer?"

She pet her cat and pulled some peanut eminems out of her pocket which she started to eat.

"They are linked together you see. What I saw is that you experience a moment of true love, and than comes the pain. Beware true love, it will mean your death."

"The highest high and than the lowest low, that's depressing."

"The images were vague, but that is what I got out of them."

"Anything else?"

She waved her hands for a few moments and than coughed loud and hard.

"I'm sorry, the vision is gone."

"What? C'mon, do your little Will Ferrell thing and bring it back!"

"I'm sorry. It comes and goes."

I took a moment to gather myself.

"But it's a joke right?"

I was expecting her to give me a wink or smile, but she just sat there with a stone cold expression.

"I'm never wrong", she said simply.

The words repeated back in my head. I'm never wrong. I'm never wrong. I'm never wrong.

I looked at Pebbles who was looking at me with sympathetic eyes. I nodded and stood from the table and walked outside of the tent.

I caught up with Vanessa and Ricky, who were in the middle of a conversation.

"I'm not saying we have to spend the night there. I just want to see the song that Sam and David are working on."

I hadn't known that Sam and David were musicians. I looked at Vanessa's who looked a little stressed.

"I thought you were coming over my house?"

I shuddered at the thought of them at her house. I could only hope that they did nothing but play monopoly and watch movies.

"Look, we can do that tomorrow night. They've been asking me to hear this song all day."

She put her hands on her waist and for some reason looked over at me for a moment. I looked away, pretending that I hadn't been paying close attention to their argument.

"Fine", she said finally, "Go ahead, I have to take Anthony home anyways."

Ricky shot me a suspicious look for a split second, but it quickly transformed into a smile as he walked towards me.

"Anthony, take care of my girl alright?"

"Sure."

"Hey, you think if I swing by Pizza Village you can hook me up?"

"I think some leftover anchovies can be arranged."

Ricky walked over to Vanessa and kissed her on the cheek. Then him, Dave, and Sam, made like a pack of wolves and scattered off.

I slowly made my way to Vanessa.

"Wow, your shirt is totally not matching your jeans." I said looking at her outfit.

She immediately looked down at her clothes and than threw her hands in the air.

"What??"

"Just a little levity, possibly misfired."

She punched me lightly on the shoulder.

"You know what I could go for? A funnel cake."

This was a hungry girl.

She was chewing on the funnel cake a few minutes later, and looking at her watch.

"I can't believe him."

"Ricky? Yeah, he really does need to shave those sideburns."

"What? No, I mean I can't believe how insensitive he is."

"He's a guy. We're not emotional creatures."

"You're not emotional?"

"I'm just a guy. We grow on trees. Well I'll give myself a little bit more credit than that. I at least grow on a palm tree, or an apple tree, one that has green apples."

We stopped walking and she looked at her phone.

"We should go."

"Right, I do have to get up early in the morning and watch cartoons."

"Did you have fun tonight?"

"I sure did. I rode the Ferris wheel with Edna which is something I've always wanted to do."

"Do you have to work tomorrow?"

"Duty calls."

"I was hoping we could hang out again soon. But I understand that you're busy with work and everything."

"There isn't enough pizza dough on the planet to keep us apart."

She laughed and grabbed my arm.

"You really are a nice guy."

If only being nice was enough.

I thought back to the prophecy I had received that night.

Hopefully it was all a sham.

Then again, you heard her. Madamme Craziel was never wrong.

8

I admit to watching a few too many horror movies during my youth. My parents had no restrictions, allowing to me watch Friday the 13th at an age when most of my friends were watching Toy Story. Still, I never once believed in any of the ghosts or demons that I saw in the movies. How could I? Nobody goes through life with any real expectation that something supernatural is lying around the corner. And it's a perfectly justified way of thinking because that kind of paranormal activity almost never happens. It was almost the same with me.

With practically the studying equivalent of a master's degree in horror movies, I should have at least noticed the signs. They say they come in all shapes and sizes. Maybe it's a bit of irony from a higher power that life's big moments are sprinkled with a pathway of signs that seem to warn us. Then again, maybe like me we're all only meant to take the signs serious in hindsight.

I stayed in the house for most of the next day watching all three Beverly Hills Cop movies. I was a sucker for anything Eddie Murphy had done in the eighties. I also tried to get started on a new movie script. My parents were at work. I had the day off from Pizza Village, and it was time to think about the future. Hollywood, screenplays, the life. I wasn't going to Hollywood any time soon, but I wanted to have some scripts in my back pocket when I made my ascent.

I was unsuccessfully trying to guess the actual size of my pencil when my doorbell rang.

My first presumption was that religiously devout people from the church had come to convert me. I figured instead of getting into an argument about religion, I'd simply not answer the door.

The doorbell rang four times over the next two minutes. Persistent people weren't they?

I walked to the front door and opened it.

There in front of me, stood a group of little girls with hearts of gold and boxes of cookies sitting in their hands. The hearts of gold was an estimation based on their uncanny smiles, the likes of which could melt the coldest man's heart. They couldn't have been more than seven or eight years old and they just screamed youthful exuberance. I was instantly taken back to my college days when I too was also happy without reason, a feeling that had not been easily replicated in the last few weeks.

I knew it was cookies, because let's be honest, what else could it be? I doubted that insurance companies had begun using little kids as a door to door gimmick. It warmed my soul to see the girl-scout tradition continue in a world where tradition seemed to be slowly getting phased out.

"Well hello there", I said in my best mature sounding voice.

"Hello sir', one of the girls answered with a sweet tone.

"What can I do for you ladies?" I asked.

One of the girl scouts stepped to the front, as if she was their spokesperson and leader. It made sense, every group had a leader. This blonde haired girl had her hair tied in a pony tail and was wearing perhaps a little bit too much make up considering her age. Her cheeks were so pink that she resembled one of the Powerpuff girls. I also noticed that she was carrying a purse. The other kids all had boxes, but being the leader must of meant that she was in charge of carrying the cash.

"Sir, we're selling cookies in order to raise money for charity."

I know everybody says they want to donate money to charity, but I truthfully did. I disapproved of the charities where you put change in a bowl at the grocery store, because you never knew where that money was going. For all I knew, at the end of the day all the cashiers would empty those change bowls into their pockets. I always wanted to donate money to a legit charity, but the opportunity had never been right in front of my face. Perhaps that was about to change.

"I would love to help you girls out. Can I just ask, what is the charity"?

I looked at the little girls, who in turn all looked at each other with blank expressions. The spokesperson didn't hesitate to tell me the truth.

"Sir, we don't know what the charity is."

"It's alright. I understand you girls are young. Did they tell you guys what a charity is"?

They all shook their heads. I guess it was time for a little tutorial.

"Well the main idea behind charity is to give back to people who may be less fortunate than you. Whether it's them having lesser wealth, or lesser health, the bottom line is it's all about giving them a little piece of what you have in order to cheer them up."

I looked at them to see if they understood what I was saying. Three of them still looked completely lost, two of them nodded their head, and two others looked like they were about to fall asleep.

The spokesperson, though, was all business.

"Sir, would you like to buy our cookies"?

You had to admire her determination.

"Little lady, I would certainly be happy to buy your cookies."

I pulled out my wallet. Perfect, I had a ten dollar bill that I could use to get a few boxes and put some real smiles on their faces.

"How much is one box?" I asked.

The spokesperson unzipped her purse; it really was a cute purse.

"One box will be nine dollars", she said softly.

These little girls were trying to hustle me.

No, wait, this was me overreacting. It was early in the morning, I'm sure I just heard her wrong.

"How much was that?"

This time she leaned forward as she spoke.

"Nine dollars", she said simply.

Yes, my initial thought was correct. They were con artists, only a step above the kids from the Village of the Damned.

Here was my dilemma. I wanted to tell them that I was short on cash, but every single last one of them had seen me pull the ten dollar bill out of my pocket. They would be yelling at me "liar, liar, pants on fire" if I tried to pull that obvious of a ruse on them.

"Well, ok." I forced a smile as I handed the spokesperson a ten dollar ball and told her to keep the change. "You know back when I was a kid, we used to be able to get three or four boxes for nine dollars. But it's a different time now, I can understand that. Do you guys have Thin Mints?"

They looked perplexed as they shook their heads.

"Thin Mints are my favorites, but it's ok. Do you guys have those chocolate dipped granola cookies"?

Now they looked absolutely puzzled. Maybe the cookies that I used to love had gone out of style?

"Well, what do you girls have?"

The spokesperson was handed a box by what appeared to be her second in command. I waited with a probing expression as she un-wrapped the black box and pulled a black plastic bag out. The cookies were concealed as if they were a top secret government weapon.

"These are the cookies we have."

She handed me the bag, and I opened it slowly, not knowing what to expect. I pulled out one of the cookies that the girl scouts were trying to sell me. The realization of what I was looking at made me giggle out loud.

"This is an Oreo", I said with a snicker.

The spokesperson shrugged as she said "Yes sir."

It was in fact a whole bag of Oreos.

"Are you sure you girls have the right box?"

She nodded.

"I've never heard of girl scouts selling Oreos. But I guess it is a down economy."

They looked at me impatiently.

"Miss Olsen gave us these and said if we don't sell them we won't get dessert tonight", the spokesperson complained.

"But they're Oreos!" I howled a little bit louder than I should have. "I can go to   Giant and probably get four of these for the same price."

That response wasn't met with much empathy from the girl scouts.

They didn't care about my financial situation. They cared about not getting Rocky Road Ice Cream that night if they didn't come home with the green. I looked at them, and one of them actually looked like she was about to start sobbing.

So I did what any respectable person would do. I purchased a box of Oreos for nine dollars.

Turns out, it wasn't even regular Oreos, they were double stuffed. What that meant was that you could only eat about three of them before you teeth cringed together and your mouth pleaded for mercy. I bid them well and closed the door.

I returned to my seat at the table. As I looked down, I noticed that it was now almost if the blank piece of paper was staring at me, pleading for me to write something, anything. Was I a writer with no imagination? No, my imagination hadn't let me down in the past. I was simply in a rut, suffering from something that I didn't want to admit too.

Writer's block, I clearly had it, but just admitting it was painful. It was kryptonite for a writer. I could deal with anything else, but having my creativity being conquered by something unknown just tore me up inside.

What was the solution? I bought a book once that was supposed to provide the answers. You could meditate in order to try to get your mind going, which usually involved sitting Indian style in a circle while the room glowed with scented candles. I had no idea where the candles were. There were all sorts of mental exercises that had helped some people in the past, but for me writer's block was psychological in a personal way.

In the past, I had resorted to thinking about the endless possibilities of fame and fortune that writing could bring. Monetary success wasn't my primary motivation for writing, but it was a dreamy goal that went with it. I was no different from the thousands of Americans who grew up wanting to make a living doing whatever it is they loved to do.

Maybe I just needed a snack to get my mind going.

I stood up and walked to the kitchen counter which was located just right of the dishwasher. This was a fairly expensive house that Lou had bought 30 years ago.

There was a row of hazel colored, wooden cabinets next to the kitchen window. Two of them were used for plates and glasses, and than there was what essentially served as a snack cabinet. Along time ago it would have undoubtedly been filled with delightful treats such as Twinkies, Slim Jims, and Pop Tarts. Now, I wasn't so sure what to expect. It seemed the more I had aged, the fewer snacks I found in the house. I opened up my kitchen cabinet and the first thing I saw almost hurt my eyes upon sight. Sitting there on the top shelf was a box of regular Oreos.

I had paid nine dollars for a box of Oreos when I already had an unopened package in the cabinet.

Damn.

I heard a brief knocking on my door just than.

On the front porch I found no trace of a human being, but there was a piece of paper lying still against the door.

I picked it up, read it, and almost choked on the Oreo I was eating.

"STAY AWAY FROM HER!"

9

"Anthony, you're late."

I looked at Sam and didn't know what to say.

"What do you mean? You called and said be here at six."

"Listen kid, don't you know by now that when I tell you to be here at six I really want you to be here at five forty five. You have to read between the lines!"

He used the apron in his hands to blow his nose.

"That makes zero sense."

He laughed hysterically. "Zero sense for somebody who is a zero. At least now I know not to trust your instincts. From now on you should show up a half an hour early, alright?"

He handed me an apron.

"What do I need an apron for?"

"Jenny called in sick, so I'm going to need you in the kitchen doing the cooking for a while."

"Then who will be on delivery"?

"We can't worry about delivery right now. We have tons of people coming in. We'll just tell people that our delivery service is temporarily unavailable."

I headed over to the kitchen, which reeked of Sam's oregano induced pizza sauce.

Once you start making pizzas non stop it seems like time flies by. I was spacing out mentally, thinking about everything that had taken place in the last few days. My co workers were all far too old to actually want to engage in consistent conversation.

I worked in the kitchen for about two hours before Sam came storming in.

"Anthony, I need you back on delivery."

"Yes sir."

He threw a piece of paper at me.

"Remember, you can't take more than thirty minutes or else the pizza is free."

"I know."

I unraveled the piece of paper and looked at it.

One Large Veggie. - Dale Bridge Cemetery

This would have been high on anybody's strange-O-meter.

"Hey Sam. I don't know if you noticed, but this delivery is addressed to the Dale Bridge Cemetery."

He looked at me without much expression.

"So what's your point"?

"Well, it's a cemetery."

"Yes, I'm so happy that we hired somebody who went to college and can read."

"But who is ordering pizza from the cemetery? Am I delivering it to one of the gravestones or something?"

"The guy on the phone said he was the caretaker."

"Caretaker? They still have those?"

"Yeah they do. And apparently he needs the crunchy taste of a veggie pizza. So that means we have to get it to him in less than thirty minutes."

My instincts told me that I should avoid the cemetery considering the prophecy that had fallen upon me.

"Listen Sam, I do allot of things for you, but going to the Cemetery at night by myself to deliver pizza to a caretaker might asking too much of me this time."

"If you want to get paid, you have to make these deliveries. If it makes you feel better, get somebody to go with you."

That wasn't a bad idea.

"Hey Vanessa, are you busy?"

"I'm watching Seinfeld."

"That's a funny show. Listen, what are you doing in about ten minutes?"

"I'll still be watching Seinfeld."

"Right. How would you like to take a little ride?"

"Anthony, you sound strange, what's going on?"

"I'm at work, and I have this delivery to make, to the cemetery. I just thought it might be fun if you came with me."

"The cemetery doesn't sound like fun."

"Well regardless, I have to deliver it."

"Why can't somebody else?"

"I'm the main delivery guy."

"Oh."

"Can you go or what?"

There was a short silence.

"Ok, I'll be ready in fifteen."

After a quick stop to fill the tank up, I was on my way to Vanessa's house. Luckily, it was right on the way to the cemetery. I pulled up to her curb and beeped the horn.

She hopped into the passenger seat a minute later. I noticed she was wearing less make-up than usual.

"What do you got there", I asked as I looked at the object in her right hand.

"I brought a flashlight and batteries. The cemetery might be pretty dark."

"Good thinking"

I drove off from her house.

"Are you nervous?" I asked as we came to a red light

"Why should I be nervous? You're the delivery boy, not me."

"Yeah but you've seen horror movies. Whoever tags along usually gets axed first."

"How comforting."

I turned the air condition on and leaned back in my seat.

"So, how is Ricky?"

"He's fine. Have you met any new girls at the video store?"

"I'm surprised that you're so interested."

"I like to keep up with the girls in your life."

"I didn't know you cared."

"I'm sure if the number ever exceeds the amount of fingers on my left hand, I'll stop caring."

"Are you implying that you have more fingers on you're left hand than you're right?"

"You're so goofy", she said as she turned on the radio. An old country song that I couldn't name blasted through my speakers.

"I love this song, don't you?" Vanessa asked

"Not so much. What did you do all day?"

"Just packing, getting everything ready."

"California, don't wake me up if I'm dreaming."

"What?"

"It's an old television show."

The dark sky seemed to get blacker as we closed in on the cemetery. I saw one small light shining bright in the outskirts. Eerie as it seemed, the cemetery seemed to be completely deserted, away from anything that could be described as civilization.

"So this is it", Vanessa said as we pulled into what could only be described as an otherwise empty two spot parking lot.

"I guess the caretaker doesn't drive", I suggested.

"Maybe he's an environmentalist."

"Captain Planet turned caretaker? I don't think so."

I turned the ignition off as Vanessa looked at me. "So what now?"

"Well I'm going to have get out of the car and give the pizza to somebody. Whoever it is better have a tip."

"And what are you going to do if he doesn't?"

"I'm going to kick his ass."

Vanessa looked away to hide her laughter.

"Ok, I'll probably apologize for the misunderstanding and try to sell him on our deep dish special."

"How brave of you. Let's get this over with."

I stayed seated.

"Listen, maybe you should stay in the car."

"Why would I stay in the car?"

"Well, you are a female."

"So?"

"Listen, I'm all for female rights and everything. I think your going to be an amazing chef. But let's be real, you're not Rosa Parks, or Elektra, or even Aeon Flux. There's a good chance that things could get a little dangerous."

"In that case, I better come along so that I can protect you if anything happens."

I took a deep breath. "Sure, you can be the Kevin Costner to my Whitney Houston."

We both slowly got out of the car, Vanessa with a flashlight in her hand and me with a large pizza. There was a small hill right next to the parking lot. We walked there and saw a huge array of graves.

The Dale Bridge Cemetery was monstrous in size. Vanessa flashed the light on some of the gravestones and I noted that they had graves dating back all the way to the early 1900s. The gravestones were surrounded by grass that had been stepped in many times. But it didn't look like anybody had mowed the lawn in a while.

"Are we even allowed to be here?" Vanessa wondered.

"We at least have a legit reason."

"This is creepy", Vanessa said.

"It's not that bad. Just think of a zombie movie, and then imagine instead of the zombies coming out of the grave they just stay in the graves and do nothing."

She pointed the flashlight at my eyes.

"I think zombies have to have come from somewhere, some sprinkle of reality. You've heard the stories, people have seen things."

"I know this theory you speak of. The one where entities such as zombies come from some real life incident."

"You don't believe that?"

"Not one bit. I believe all things supernatural come from somebody's creative imagination."

"And yet you have the entire Twilight Zone collection on DVD."

"Hey, fiction is still entertaining."

We walked past the gravestones which were all aligned very neatly in several different rows.

"See look", I said. "No empty graves. They're all how they should be."

"I can actually hear the trepidation in your voice."

"What?"

"The trepidation, it's usually a sign that someone is scared."

I stopped for a moment. "Hey, I'm not feeling trepi-anything, not at all. I'm calm, cool, and collected. I'm not sure if you're aware of this, but my middle name is Fonze, because I'm cool you see."

"Your middle name is Oscar."

"Now how do you know that?"

"You told me on the way to the carnival."

"Well, that was a mistake."

We resumed walking. It actually was kind of a nice night.

I stopped when my foot was suddenly sunk into the grass. I shrieked.

"What is it??" Vanessa asked.

I stopped yelling, and pulled my foot up. I looked down to see that nothing had grabbed me. I had slipped into a mud-hole. Thankfully I had somehow managed to not drop the pizza box. I reached down and pulled my foot out.

"What is it?? Are you ok??" Vanessa was asking frantically.

"Something grabbed me."

Vanessa pointed the flashlight at my jeans, which were covered in mud, and than she pointed the flashlight back at my face. "Nothing grabbed you".

I shook the dirt off my leg. "Hey, I don't know why it grabbed me, it just did. We're definitely not alone out here. You've seen the movie Tremors right?"

"Yeah."

'They're underground Vanessa. They're under the ground!"

She gave a deadpan reaction as she pointed the flashlight at the grim path ahead of us.

We walked on, as the graves around us grew by the number. We were right around the middle section of the cemetery, surrounded completely by gravestones. I went to grab her hand but she looked at me as if I was crazy. I guess she wasn't spooked at all, or at least not enough to let me hold her hand.

I started to wonder what reason was there to be scared at all. Everything seemed normal enough. It didn't have to be the souls of the dead wandering around haunting people; it could just be a normal cemetery with dead people who acted like dead people.

That's when an icy cold hand grabbed me by the back of my neck.

"What the hell?"

I turned to see a shadowy figure in a black cloak. He wore a hood over his head that masked his identity. I was immediately in awe of whoever it was, than the fear kicked in as I tried to push his hand off. He let go of my neck but grabbed me by the shoulders and threw me to the ground.

I looked at Vanessa and screamed "run". She tried, but the mystery attacker pushed her in the back and she fell also fell upon the grass.

I got to my feet and grabbed our attacker from behind but in a super quick instant he threw an elbow and caught me right in the mouth. I fell to the ground again and saw him start to move towards me. He made a grunting noise that didn't sound human as reached for my leg.

I backed up quickly, trying to avoid his hands. But I ended up backing right into a gravestone that hit me in the upper back. A gush of pain shot through me and I had nowhere to go. I froze completely as the masked figure leaned in towards me.

Closer, closer, closer.

My skin was turning cold as I saw him inches from my face. I tried to see who it was but his face was nothing but a dark menacing nothingness.

Just as he was near me I saw him stand back and put his face back in his hood. He was grabbing his face for some reason. He slowly started to back up a little bit. I looked around me and noticed the pizza box was open and right next to me. When I looked back up again the attacker was gone.

I cautiously crawled towards Vanessa who looked to be conscience.

"Are you alright?" I asked.

She seemed a little out of it as she gathered her thoughts.

"Was that the killer?" She asked.

I looked in the distance, searching for some type of clue.

"I don't know. I think so."

"Put you're hands where I can see them", I heard somebody yell behind me.

I turned to see a cop standing with a flashlight.

"Hello, is there a problem officer?" I asked casually.

The cop, a plump man with an extraordinary amount of facial hair, stood looking at us suspiciously.

"What are you two doing out here, this time of the night?"

I didn't know what to say, but luckily Vanessa had her wits.

"Officer, my friend here works for a pizza place, and somebody here ordered Veggie lovers. We're just delivering it", Vanessa said honestly.

Good thing she was there. I would have told the officer something about us hunting ghosts.

I showed the officer the pizza box, a clear indicator in his mind that we were being straight with him.

"I'm going to need to see you're license and registration."

"Sure officer, that won't be a problem at all."

I contemplated telling him about the attacker, but for some reason I didn't, and neither did Vanessa. We walked back to my car where I showed him my license, and my registration. Well I would have showed him my registration, only I couldn't find it anywhere in the car. How had it gone missing in the last week?

"I seem to have misplaced my registration", I said.

The officer flashed a light in my left eye, which seemed a little unnecessary.

"Did you just say that you misplaced you're registration?" He asked with a tone of evil curiosity.

Suddenly I felt like a drug dealer who had stolen the car and had a dead body in the trunk.

"I thought it was in my glove compartment, but it doesn't seem to be there."

I looked at Vanessa who looked far calmer than I was.

"Well that's going to be a problem."

The officer reached into his pocket, and though some part of me was expecting forty one shots, I was relieved to see him pull out a piece of paper.

"I'm going to have to give you a ticket for not having you're registration card."

"You can get a ticket for that?" I was about to say more, but the officer gave an expression indicating that any smartass remarks might get me a beating, so I elected to shut up.

He checked out my plates and my license number while Vanessa and I waited anxiously.

The cop came back to the car a minute later.

"You have a court date listed on the citation, but you can pay the fine out of court."

'Thanks officer."

"I also want to remind you that your court date for not returning rental property is in three days."

Damn Mr. Holland's Opus.

All these court costs were going to be putting me in a financial hole.

We were driving away from the cemetery a moment later.

I hopped on Bradley Road and momentarily started to relax.

"I'm sorry I invited you to come with me", I said to Vanessa.

"Look on the bright side; you get to keep the pizza."

I handed the pizza box to her. "I'm not a big Veggie guy. I'm sure your mom will enjoy it. "

"Who do you think ordered the pizza?"

"It had to be whoever attacked us."

"Do you think that was the killer?"

"I don't really know."

It was somewhere during this conversation that she leaned over and kissed me on the cheek. It was quick, and sudden, and caught me completely by surprise.

"You don't have to apologize for inviting me. That was scary, but kind of fun.'

"You like the adventure huh?"

"Something like that."

I looked up in my rear view just then and caught a glimpse of a huge pair of headlights behind us. Vanessa turned and looked back.

"What is that?" I asked.

"I think that's Ricky behind us."

I looked back but only saw the headlights.

"Why do you say that? I asked nervously.

"He drives a Black Honda Accord just like that one."

"Oh", I muttered.

"What?"

"It's nothing."

Vanessa must not have seen the television report of the murder. It was certainly something.

"There are plenty of people in town with Black Honda Accords", I offered.

"You're probably right", she said and turned back towards the front.

It was clear that she wasn't aware that her boyfriend was driving the same vehicle as the town's serial killer. I looked in the rear view mirror and finally saw that it was indeed a Black Accord. But I couldn't make out the drivers face.

"Why didn't we tell the police about the guy who attacked us?"

I looked back at Vanessa. I didn't really have an answer for her.

"I guess it slipped my mind", I lied.

"Have you noticed that every time we hang out something bad happens to us?"

CRASH!

My back suddenly flew forward and my face crashed into the steering wheel. The collision had caught me totally off guard. I turned and saw Vanessa whose head had also hit the dashboard. She was holding it in pain as we both tried to figure out what had happened.

"He hit us", she said.

I turned and saw the Honda Accord only a few inches behind us. He had rammed us from behind.

And he was coming at us again.

"Speed up", she yelled,

I applied my foot to the gas pedal hard and tried to survey our situation.

We were on a main road that had a speed limit of forty five but I pushed my Civic to seventy in an attempt to get away from the Accord.

But the Accord wasn't slowing down.

"I don't suppose he'll stop and give us his insurance information?"

"He's trying to kill us!"

"But why?"

I was hoping my speeding would draw the police but so far it looked like a long and empty road with just us and the killer right behind.

"What are we going to do?"

"Highway to the danger zone", was all I said.

My mind flashed back to the race.

Three inches too short.

I refused to let it happen again.

Seventy five miles per hour.

Eighty..

Eighty three.

Every time I sped up the killer matched my speed.

"I have to lose him".

"How are you going to do that?"

Most car chases I had seen in movies had ended with one of the cars exploding. I didn't want that to happen here, so I had to come up with a plan that was a little more realistic.

"We're on Bradley, I'm going to take two right turns in a moment which should put us on Hoadley. There is an IHOP at the end of Hoadley. There will be lots of people there."

"So we just have to make it there alive", Vanessa said solemnly.

The problem was that the killer and I were both going 85 now. From someone looking outside of their window, it looked like a race was going on in which I was given a head start.

"Oh no", Vanessa said suddenly.

"What?"

"Your gas is on E"!

If everything else wasn't bad enough, we were going to run out of gas at any second.

"Damnit!" I cried.

I kept at eighty five even though it was making the gas run out at a furious pace.

It was time to find out if the killer was from around here. The first right turn was going to be predictable, but only somebody who knew the town in and out would suspect the second right turn.

"This is going to be rough!" I screamed.

We hit the sharp right turn. I slowed down only a little bit as the turn took me almost to the opposite side of the road.

SCREEEEEEEEEEEEEEEECH.

The car was skidding out as it finally moved straight forward. I pumped my first afterwards but saw in the rear view the killer making a far smoother right turn than I had.

"Great, we have Speed Racer chasing us."

"When is the next right?" Vanessa asked.

"Here it comes."

I didn't want to slow down at all for the second right turn. I wanted it to be a complete surprise. I was down to seventy five and the killer was right behind me at eighty.

I wanted to wait until the very last second to make the turn.

"Aren't you going to slow down?? The turn is right here."

"We have to make him think we're going straight."

Vanessa leaned back in her seat and held onto her door handle.

I put both hands on the right side of the steering wheel.

If I do this too slowly than he could crash right into us.

He would be at fault, but we would be dead.

Fast and steady, I told myself.

As it looked like we were passing the turn I threw all my arm strength on the turning wheel, pushing it right as I also gently pushed down on the brakes.

Vanessa screamed as we came close to making a full three sixty spin.

Luckily, the car stabilized enough to make a turn.

I looked back and saw the Accord go straight instead of making the right.

"Yes!"

"It worked, thank goodness." Vanessa said as she let go of her door handle.

We calmed down as the IHOP soon came into sight.

"You still think that was Ricky?" I asked after I had caught my breath.

She stared out of her window for a moment and than looked over at me.

"Whoever it was, they wanted us dead."

"So what do you think?"

Robert leaned back on my couch and offered an inquisitive look. It was the day after the cemetery incident, a Friday morning. My uncle had untypically gone off for the weekend, on a retreat in the mountains.

"I think that you're in the friend zone."

"No, what do you think about what happened?"

"Oh, that. I think Ricky ordered the pizza from the cemetery. And that was probably him chasing you guys."

"But why? And how did the opera with Heather go?"

"It was great."

"I'm happy for you."

"Are you really?"

"Well I didn't want to appear self involved. What the hell am I going to do?"

"When is Vanessa leaving for California?"

"In two weeks."

He stood and began pacing around my room.

"That's not long. You may be better off just staying away."

"What do you mean?"

"Think about it. If Vanessa's boyfriend is the killer and this was a movie, than you would probably be lined up to be the next victim. Hell, you've already been attacked. And he even warned you to stay away from her."

"I know."

Robert sat back down and looked me in the eyes.

"It seems to me that you can take yourself out of the situation by simply staying away from Vanessa."

What a task that would be.

I sighed. "I don't know if I can. It's hard to explain."

"You're supposed to be a realist."

"You can be a realist and a romantic."

"No, you can't. That is an oxymoron."

"What do you think I should do? Forget that I ever met her?"

"People in the friend zone shouldn't be risking their lives for the sake of romance."

"I get what you're saying, but I'd at least like to make sure that she's not dating a killer."

"This is not going to end well."

"Are you going to help me out or what?"

"What can we do?"

"The key here is Ricky."

"How can we find out if he is the killer or not?"

"Stake out his house?"

"I don't want to do that."

"What doesn't add up is that the guy in the cemetery had me at his will but something made him back off."

"Maybe he was allergic to something?'

And with those words, it hit me.

"Eureka!"

"What?"

"I was sitting there, and the pizza was right next to me. And the box was open."

"So he's allergic to pizza?"

"No, but in every box of pizza we include a little packet of garlic sauce."

"I don't follow."

"The story you told me on graduation night."

"Vampires?"

"Why not?"

"They aren't real, that's why."

"But how do we know?"

"Are you on something?"

"I know it takes a huge leap of faith, but why else would the attacker have left me in the cemetery if not because of the garlic?"

"So you think everything with Doug is actually a true story?"

"It's possible."

"This feels like a rerun of CSI."

"Yeah but this is real life and Vanessa may be in danger here."

"You're protecting her and meanwhile she's probably over Ricky's house right now."

"Do you really have to say that?"

"Hey man, it's been that way since the beginning of time. Athletes get the girl and vampire investigators get no play!"

"Right, thanks for that information."

"Look, I don't know what the hell is going on. But, I'm with you I guess."

"Thanks. I think the only way to get the truth is to talk to Ricky."

"And what should I do?"

"We have to find out if the story is true. If there really was murders in this town than it should be documented somewhere. Can you go to the library and do some research?"

"Where is the library?"

"What?"

"Kidding. But one question. If Ricky is a vampire, and he knows you know, won't he kill you?"

I gulped.

"Probably."

11

"What is your favorite movie of all time?"

I asked Vanessa this as I stood on her porch and watched her walk outside.

"Batman."

"Really?"

"You seem surprised?"

"Most women love romance movies, your a little against the grain."

"But Batman had romance."

"I suppose so."

"Who tried to kill us Anthony?"

I had to come expect her directness, but I wasn't prepared with an answer.

"I've been thinking about that.'"

"And?"

"I don't know. I was thinking maybe you could ask Ricky?"

"You think it was him?"

"I know he's your boyfriend, but it was his car that was behind us."

"He wouldn't do anything like that."

"I believe you, but could you still ask?"

She skipped off the porch and I followed her for a few steps before she turned around.

"What's the plan for today?" She wondered.

"I don't have a clue."

"You said you wanted to do something today?"

"And I do."

"But you have no plan?"

"I wanted to see you. I figured I'd figure out the rest on the way."

"On the way to where?"

"Don't you ever get in your car and just drive?"

"No, I don't have GPS."

"I don't either, but it's still something I like to do to clear my head."

"So you want to just drive around?"

I kicked a pebble in her driveway.

"How about this. We can do something that I only normally do by myself.

"As long as it's not driving."

We were on a basketball court a few minutes later.

"This is your activity?" Vanessa looked at the basketball hoop as it she had never seen one before.

"It's a fun game."

I tossed her the basketball which she caught and than looked at me.

"Would you like to play one on one?" I asked.

"Not really."

She passed the ball back to me, which I clumsily dropped off my fingers.

"You're really good at this", she said sarcastically.

I picked up the ball and began dribbling.

"Did you ever play sports in high school?" I asked.

"Yes, Volleyball. How about you?"

"I tried out for cheerleading, but they cut me."

She walked over and tried to steal the ball from me, but I turned my back around so she couldn't reach in.

"I like the effort", I said with amusement.

"Do you come here often?' She stood up and walked towards the hoop.

"It's my sanctuary."

"I don't have one of those."

"Everybody has one. How about cooking?"

"It doesn't take my mind off the world."

"One thing my mom told me once was that the world is always the same, and the only thing that really changes is you."

" When did you become an optimist?"

"I alternate between hopeful and hopeless."

"How long have you been writing?"

"Since I can remember. It's not always good though. Sometimes I get lost in being the observer and forget to be the participant."

I shot a jump shot that rimmed out. Vanessa grabbed the rebound and started to dribble in place.

"It's not so hard." She said.

"Maybe the WNBA will offer you a scholarship."

"Ricky made me race him."

"Did you win?"

"No"

"At least you came in second place."

"Your very glass half full today."

"I think the glass is about two thirds full."

She took a jump shot that bounced off the top off the backboard. The ball rolled next to my leg and I picked it up.

"They just retracted your scholarship."

"Why don't we get something to eat?"

"Your appetite is quite eternal."

12

My doorbell rang the next day.

I opened it and saw Ricky Winston standing with a briefcase in his hands.

"Hey Anthony, can I come in?"

"Sure."

We walked over to my living room where we both took a seat on my couch.

"I was kind of surprised to hear from you Anthony. Are you really looking for car insurance?"

I smiled. "Yeah, of course. My rates are way too high."

"Well, you are a young driver. Do you have any speeding tickets on your record?"

"I had two of them in college. I was coming from IHOP and the cop was waiting, you know, trying to hit his monthly quota."

"It happens to all of us."

"I'm kind of surprised that you work with car insurance, after being a racer and all."

"Man, all of that almost feels like a past lifetime."

"It was a long time ago, I agree."

"I think my company should be able to get you a better rate. I'm just going to need to get some information on your driving record and your car."

"Hey have you seen Vanessa lately?"

I tried to slip in Vanessa's name without seeming to be concerned about it. He didn't seem to mind talking about her.

"We went and saw a movie last night actually."

"That's nice."

I figured that she hadn't told him about our little cemetery adventure. He would have asked me about it if he knew.

"If you don't mind me asking, how did you guys meet?" I again tried to make it sound casual.

"Vanessa? I was with my friends at Dairy Queen and she came in to get a Banana Split. I started talking to her. She was new in town and didn't know anybody so we went from there."

It was just his luck that he had met her first.

"So you met at a video store?" He asked me curiously.

"Yeah, we were both going after the same movie. Than she needed jumper cables."

I wanted to make it seem like circumstances had made Vanessa and I friends instead of me pursuing her.

"You know she's leaving right?" He asked with a noticeably down tone.

"Yeah, California."

He turned serious suddenly.

"I'm going to miss her. You know, after I hurt my knee, I hated my life for a while".

"Really?"

I hadn't expected Ricky to be so open with me.

"I was totally suicidal for a while. I just kept asking myself, why me? Why was I given the talent and physical abilities if I wasn't going to be able to use it? You ever have been so down that you just wanted to end things?"

He was being so honest that I couldn't help but open up myself.

"Actually, yes. You know, while you were busy being a hero in high school, I was busy sinking into depression."

He seemed surprised by my confession.

"Hey man, if I was ever a jerk to you in high school, I apologize."

It was surreal to be having the school jock apologize to me for my own miserable high school experience. I almost forgot why I had invited him there.

"Have you asked Vanessa to stay?"

He looked down at his briefcase and than looked back up.

"It's what she wants to do. If my knee had been healthy I wouldn't have wanted anybody telling me not to pursue my dream."

"It's funny, it seems like women always have more realistic dreams. They want to be nurses or chefs, practical things. Guys dream about being star athletes and filmmakers, sometimes we're unrealistic."

He nodded and we sat there. And than he caught me a little off guard.

"Anthony, you like her, don't you?"

And just like that, the mood changed from guys bonding to guys competing.

"What? Why do you say that?" I played dumb but Ricky wasn't having it.

"I'm not a fool man. Why else would you ask me over today? I'm not buying the idea that you take insurance serious enough to have a one on one meeting."

"You knew I was up to something from the beginning? Why didn't you say something earlier?"

"I was just making sure. But I knew you didn't want to be friends. I was first suspicious when I saw you at the carnival. I was thinking, what are the odds of me seeing this guy again? I figured you must still be better about losing that race to me, but I still didn't know what your angle was. Now with your questions about Vanessa, I know the real deal. "

"Alright, I guess there is no point in denying it. I have a thing for Vanessa."

My confession simmered for a moment. I didn't know how Ricky would react. He could have started a fight with me, but it was doubtful since we were in my house.

"Have you told her this?"

"No, should I?"

The confidence that I had always seen suddenly returned to Ricky.

"It wouldn't get you very far."

"Well, than none of this will be a problem. A woman always has free will to make a choice."

"One thing I have to know. Do you really care about her or is this just a way to get back to me for the race?"

"The race is ancient history. Besides, I fell for Vanessa before I even knew she had a boyfriend."

He stood from the couch.

"Stay away from her", he said suddenly.

"Dream another dream."

He walked to the door before turning around.

"What is it about you and me? First you challenge me to a race, and now this? Do you know what they say about history repeating itself?"

He opened the door. I scratched my chin and nodded.

"Maybe these are just the roles we were meant to play."

With that, he smiled and walked away.

Robert called me a few minutes after Ricky left.

"Anthony, you're not going to believe this".

"You found something?"

"An article, it's just like the story I told you."

"Really?"

"Yeah. It talks about the murders and than what happened when Doug tried to bite Jessica. The only difference is that Doug may not have died. The cops came in and shot him, and than they took him to the hospital. It doesn't say what happened to him after that."

"So if Doug is a vampire he could still be alive?"

"Yes. Did you find out anything about Ricky?"

"I talked to him a little, and I don't think he's our vampire."

"Are you sure? Did you look in his eyes?"

"Yes. I imagine that a vampire would be an absolutely wonderful liar, but all I saw was a guy in love."

"Ouch. I guess they're relationship is more serious than you expected?"

"He cares about her. I can't see him ever hurting her."

"There is still a killer in Dale Bridge, somebody who is after you."

"I know, but Ricky was our only lead. And I don't think we have enough evidence to approach the police. They would probably think that we're the killers."

So where does the investigation go from here?"

"Nowhere. Ricky was pretty much it. If somebody wants to kill me, I'm not hard to find."

"And Vanessa?"

"I don't know. When I go with the flow I end up miserable, and when I try to make something happen, I end up miserable. How is that possible? You know, I grew up watching a whole bunch of movies where the guy gets the girl and lives happily ever after. But that's not realistic. Classic American literature is far more real. Did Gatsby get the girl? No. Pip? Nope. Scarlett? No way."

"There is something else you should know", Robert said, interrupting my rant.

"What?"

"That night that Doug tried to bite the girl. Tomorrow will be exactly forty years ago."

"What?"

"Yeah. I just looked at the date on the article."

"That can't be a coincidence."

I suddenly knew who we needed to talk too.

"What are we going to do?" Robert asked.

"I'll tell you on the way."

"On the way where?"

"To Don Cramer's house."

It wasn't hard finding Don's address in the phone book.

"I just want to find out more about what he knows."

"Don sounds like a nut job."

I had filled Robert in on what had happened that day in jail and the night when I found Don in the bushes.

"That's what I thought originally. But what he said is starting to make more sense."

"Let's hope not. We have a much better chance dealing with a human killer and not one of the undead."

I shuddered at the thought.

We walked to Don's porch but neither of us rung the doorbell.

"What are we waiting for?" Robert asked.

"It's kind of late isn't it?"

Robert looked at his watch. "It's only eight."

I jumped off the porch and stood in the front yard. I looked up at the house and saw that all the lights were off except for the top left bedroom. It was strange for all the lights to be off at eight, but I didn't think much of it.

"That has to be Don's room."

"Maybe it's his parents watching a movie."

"Let's throw a small pebble at the window."

"What?"

"Yeah, he'll hear it and come out."

"Or his parents will come out and yell at us."

"It's better than ringing the doorbell and waking everybody in the house up."

"Fine', Robert said. "Be my guest."

I picked up a pebble and held it steady. I had to be careful to throw it hard enough to make a noise but not hard enough for it to crack the glass.

"Here goes nothing", I said as I drew my hand back.

I launched the pebble with what I thought was just the right amount of force.

It hit the bedroom window and made quite the boom as Robert looked at me and shook his head.

"I guess we're about to find out whose in that room".

It took us only a moment to see a figure appear in the bedroom window.

Luckily, it was Don. He looked down at us for a second without expression and than held up his index figure before disappearing.

A minute later he opened his front door and joined us in the front yard.

"Hey brother, what are you doing here?"

"Don, how are you doing?"

"I was just in the house watching the tube. What's up?'

"Listen, you remember that conversation we had a few nights ago?

He looked at Robert and than back at me.

"It's cool, that's my friend Robert. I told him everything."

"Yeah I remember the other night."

'Well, I need to talk to you about it a little bit more in detail."

He leaned in and a new excitement took his face.

"You saw one of them didn't you?"

"No, well yes, I don't know, maybe. Something attacked me in a cemetery."

"What were you doing in a cemetery?"

"Delivering a pizza."

"Typical. What makes you think it wasn't a human who attacked you?"

"Well he had me trapped, but I think it was the garlic sauce from the pizza that made him back off."

Don smiled, as if he had been validated by my words.

"Vampires are allergic to garlic, of course!"

"But why did a vampire attack me?"

Don scratched his head.

"Vampires don't do anything without a reason. He must want

something from you."

"I think I want to hear more about this vampire."

He nodded. "Alright, but not here. Can we go back to your place?"

"Sure."

We drove to my house. Lou was still out of town so we had the place to ourselves.

"So what got you involved in this?'" I asked Don.

He looked at Robert and me and took a deep breath.

"I saw a girl murdered."

Robert looked at me in disbelief.

"You saw Becky get murdered?"

"I was out walking one night, coming from a friend's house. It was dark; the moon was full, I had gotten some poison ivy that day and it was killing me! Brother I tried all types of cream to get rid of the itch."

"Yes but about the vampire."

"Oh right. I'm walking through the park and that's when I see her on a park bench with some guy".

"What guy?"

"At first I didn't recognize him. I knew I had seen him before but I couldn't place his face."

"But you tried breaking into his house later on, right?"

"It was later on that I matched the face with a name in my old high school yearbook."

"So you know who it is?"

"Yes."

I sighed.

"So he saw you that night?"

"Not at first. I was behind a bush, watching them. The girl seemed uncomfortable and he seemed overly confident. I wanted to see if he was going to make a move."

"So what happened?" Robert asked.

"They started kissing, like really hard, intense kissing. And than the guy opened his eyes and started looking around. It was like he was trying to make sure there was nobody watching."

"And he still didn't see you?"

"No, I'm good at not being seen. I just stood there, motionless. Than I saw him start to change."

"Change?"

"He totally morphed into something vicious brother. His eyes turned pink, and they just got wider and more intense, like much more focused. And than he opened his mouth, and I saw his teeth. They started to grow."

"Oh wow", Robert mumbled.

"His teeth turned into fangs!"

"And than what?"

"He bit her man, leaned in and started sucking her blood. And I screamed."

Don stood from the chair and walked towards the window.

"He saw me than. We made eye contact, he saw me clear as day. He let go of her and stood from the park bench and started walking towards me. So I just got up and ran all the way home."

"And that's why he's after you?"

"I don't think, I know. I'm a witness. I did some research and figured out how to kill vampires, so that's what I was trying to do when the police caught me for trespassing. I couldn't tell them the truth. I don't think they would believe anything about a vampire."

"This is crazy." Robert remarked.

"Alright", I said. "We have to know. Who is the vampire? Whose house did you break into?"

He leaned in.

"His name is Ricky Winston."

Robert looked at me with a shocked expression. I could only match it. I guess Don had gone to my high school.

"Listen; if you saw Ricky in person you could identify him as the vampire right?"

"Sure, I'll never forget that face. But I don't want to go anywhere near him."

Robert put his hand up. "How can it can be Ricky? You used to see him at school right?"

"He didn't have to be a vampire during school. He could have become one after graduation."

"How?"

"Well', Don replied. "Somebody would have had to bit him, like another Vampire."

"So", I surmised, "If Ricky just became a vampire, than he's not the Doug from your story. That vampire has obviously been here a while. So there may be two total vampires, if not more."

"Than this town is completely screwed", Robert said to nobody in particular. "Why do we even want to be involved?"

I bit my lip.

"Whoever this is has alread killed, and if we don't do anything, he could easily kill again. And there is the little fact that he's already attempted to kill me, remember?"

Don seemed anxious. "What's the plan brother?"

I thought about it. "In the movies, if you kill the head vampire, than all the other vampires turn back to human, right?" I looked to Don for confirmation.

"That sounds like Invasion of the Body Snatchers. Are you sure you're not thinking of aliens?"

"I could have sworn I saw it in at least one vampire movie."

"We don't even know who the head vampire is", Robert complained.

"Let's start with Ricky."

"And you're sure you don't want to kill him simply because he's dating the girl your in love with?"

"I never said I was in love with her."

For the first time, the idea of killing Ricky was starting to become prominent in my mind.

"Listen, Don, if we're going to kill him, we absolutely need you to identify him one more time. Otherwise we may be killing a human being which I don't think any of us want on our record."

"Are we sure we want to do this?" Robert asked.

We all let that question hang in the air for a few moments. If nobody objected, it was all over for Ricky. The truth was that Robert and I still had no concrete evidence that vampires existed. Don had seen one, but what did we really know about Don Cramers? I spoke up only because nobody else would.

"How about this. We'll bring garlic with us. Once Don identifies him we can try to throw garlic on him and see if it affects him. If he's a vampire, we stake him. And if he's not, we'll claim we were drunk."

"Alright brother. Let's do it. But not tonight."

"What's wrong with tonight?" I asked.

"I got court in the morning brother, for the trespassing."

"Fine, but we have to do it tomorrow night. It's the anniversary. I have a feeling our vampire is planning something big."

"Alright brother. Everybody get a good night sleep."

14

With Uncle Lou out of town, I was expecting a relatively quiet night. After all, I needed to be well rested physically and mentally in order to get ready for the big vampire slaying that was looking to happen the next night.

At the same time, I started to have paranoid thoughts about Vanessa being alone with Ricky.

What if he was the vampire? Was it safe for to leave her alone with him?

I decided to go to her house, just to check on her and make sure everything was alright.

Maybe it was just a subconscious reason I had given myself to go see her.

The trip didn't take long; soon I was standing in front of her house.

I walked up the yard, but before I got into the door I decided to look through the living room window.

And that's when I knew I had made a mistake.

They were kissing.

No big deal, right? That's part of what a boyfriend does with his girlfriend.

So why did it hurt so much?

I turned from the window and walked back to my car.

If this was a race, than Ricky had basically had a huge head start. How could I compete?

The negative mindset was coming back. I tried to push it away but it was very persistent.

I was asking myself far too many questions that didn't have answers.

When I got back to my house, I took a seat on my own couch and turned on an old REO Speedwagon album. "I can't fight this feeling" played throughout the living room.

I hadn't lost and yet I was already accepting defeat. I was lost in the lyrics when my doorbell rang.

I was more than surprised by who was standing there.

"Vanessa, I didn't know you were coming here."

"I wanted to see you."   "Oh", I replied.

"Didn't you get my text message?"

I had turned my phone off an hour earlier.

"No, but it's quite alright. Come on in."

She walked in, the first time she had been in my house. She peered around curiously but not critically. Than she took a seat in the living room.

"Are you ok?" I asked her.

"Not really."

I brought her a glass of water. There was something a little bit off about her.

"So you want to talk about it?"

I was a bit thrown off by the whole situation. I had always seen her strength, and only a glimpse of her vulnerability. Now it was out and about, parading around my living room.

She leaned forward on my couch and looked directly down at the floor.

"I had an argument with Ricky", she said a moment later.

"Does he know about our cemetery escapades?"

"No. I asked him what he was doing that night and he said he was over his friend Sam's house. I believe him."

"I'm glad you guys have such a trusting relationship."

She looked at me.

"We broke up."

"Oh."

"We just agreed that it wasn't going to work out since I was leaving."

"How do you feel about that?"

She cleared a tear from her eye.

"I don't know. Everything is so fickle."

"That's an interesting word."

She took a few sips of water.

"I tend to shy away from letting people get close to me."

"It's understandable."

"This must sound terrible to you. I don't mind having lots of friends, but there are always limitations."

"You don't get emotionally attached to people. I can see the good in that."

"I hate that about me."

"Everybody is flawed. I sometimes fall for people too quickly."

"That's not a flaw."

"It is what it is. So why did you come over here?"

"I was making a shrimp cocktail at my house and I just became really depressed."

"You can't blame yourself for the break up. You have to go where your dream is."

"What is your dream?"

"I try not to dream. But I can tell you that a short while ago I was completely lost. It was hard for me to find any purpose in every day life."

"How did you get out of that mindset?"

"Honestly? I threw myself into arts and crafts."

"What?"

"No I'm kidding."

I didn't want to keep lying to her. But the only alternative was the truth. I thought to myself, maybe it would set me free. And, we'll all be dead in seventy years anyways.

I took in allot of air and tried to relax. The truth was a bit heavy.

"What I did was meet you."

She didn't respond so I continued.

"Listen, maybe I'm not the person you should be talking too about this. You were expecting a friend"

"No, it's fine. I appreciate your honesty."

"You can try one of those 1-800 numbers. They always work for me."

"Hey, where is your uncle?"

"He's gone for a few days."

We were both sitting on the couch. I was fidgeting with my fingers for no apparent reason. I looked down at Vanessa's wrist, and as usual saw her grandmother's bracelet shining back at me.

"That bracelet means a lot to you doesn't it?"

She put her hand on it.

"It means everything."

"Did you know your grandmother?"

"She died before I was born. I would always look at her pictures and wonder what she was like. And than when I was fourteen my mom gave me the bracelet. She said my grandmother would have wanted me to have it."

"I think your grandmother would have been very proud of you. You're going to be a world famous chef after all."

"Perhaps."

"Hey, you don't need me to cheer you up. Pretty soon you'll be in Texas learning how to make everything from lobster to Asian cuisine. And I'll still be here, eating Lean Cuisine TV dinners."

"You're wrong. I do need you to cheer me up; you have a gift for it."

"I do?"

"Sure. You always know what to say to make me laugh."

The gift and the curse, I thought. The funny guy could only make it so far.

She looked at me for a moment without blinking. I didn't know what to make of it.

"What are you thinking Anthony?"

"I was wondering if being happy is just a temporary thing."

" You just have to find what makes you happy and make it stick."

"But what if that thing moves to California?"

A smile strolled across her face.

"Anthony, I could both laugh and cry right now."

We stared at each for a moment; there were no words necessary. I noticed my arm was on her leg but I didn't remember when I had put it there. She leaned in just as she had done at the gas station.

This time, I was a little bit more cautious.

"Listen, I don't want us to kiss just to make you feel better in the moment."

"I want you to kiss me because we both will enjoy it. There is no other motive behind it."

I tried to continue being logical although she was looking prettier by the second.

"But what will it mean for the future?"

"I don't know. I can't tell you what I'll eat for breakfast tomorrow. I'm only worried about the here and now."

I nodded slowly. "I'll probably have waffles and turkey sausage tommorrow, with a side of strawberries and..."

She kissed me in mid sentence.

She was right about one thing. Everything was fickle.

We were interrupted by a knocking at my door a moment later.

15

"Don, this isn't the best time."

He was standing there with his usually excited smile as he nervously scratched his left leg.

"Anthony, I need a place to stay/"

"What? Why?"

"The Vampire, he's after me."

"Right now?"

"Yeah, on the way home from your house I saw him. The same one from the park. He was just smiling at me. I pushed his hand off me and ran. And he chased me all the way over here."

"Well", I looked back at Vanessa on the couch. "Can't you come back in a half an hour?"

"No!"

I sighed. "Alright, fine."

I let him in.

"I have to tell you something brother."

"What is it?"

He leaned in and spoke quietly.

"The guy who chased me, Ricky, he was wearing a Milton High Track team jersey."

I took a moment to process that while Don walked over to the living room where Vanessa was.

"Hi, I'm Don Cramers. And you are?"

She shot a surprised glance at me.

"I'm Vanessa."

"It's nice to meet you."

He stared at her for a prolonged moment. I waited patiently until he looked back at me.

"So what are you two up too?" He smirked as I walked back into the living room.

"Oh, nothing much."

"Hey Anthony, does she know?"

"Know what?" Vanessa asked curiously.

"Well I..."

"About the vampires", Don interrupted me.

"Listen Don, I don't know if we should be throwing that word around."

"What do you mean Vampires?" Vanessa asked.

"I'll tell you all about it." Don took a seat next to her on the couch.

He spent the next few minutes telling her about his experience with the undead. She sat, wide-eyed, turning to look at me every few sentences or so. Luckily, and just by pure coincidence, Don left out the part about how we were suspecting Ricky of being the vampire. They had just broken up; I didn't know how she would have taken it if we confessed that we were planning on staking Ricky through the heart the next day.

"There is a vampire outside?" Vanessa sounded worried.

"I don't know if he's still there. He was behind me when I got to the door."

"Well, thank you for bringing a vampire to my house Don. That was especially considerate of you."

"What are we going to do?" Vanessa asked.

"We don't have to do anything", I answered.

"I don't want to go home if a vampire is waiting outside."

"If it will ease your worries, I have the house to myself and you're welcome to stay".

Don stood up, "Thanks Anthony! The three of us will have a hell of a good time!"

It wasn't what I had in mind but I guess we were in for a good old fashioned slumber party.

We spent the next two hours watching 'The Hangover' on DVD. And than we played the board game 'Scene It'. When that was over, I tried to call it a night.

"So what are the sleeping arrangements looking like?" Don asked.

"You can have the couch", I offered.

"It can't be any worse than the bushes."

"Vanessa?"

"I'll sleep in your room."

"Oh."

"Do you have a mattress?"

I should have known better.

"Yeah, I'll set up a little bed for you."

Soon I was lying in my bed while Vanessa lay on the mattress I had set up on the floor. I quietly stood off the bed and walked to the window. This was a problem for me sometimes, not being able to sleep. My introspective ways sometimes led to insomnia.

I stared outside, half expecting to see a vampire. The most horrific things are never so obvious. I saw nothing but the dead street outside.

I turned and saw Vanessa curled up on the mattress. She was perfectly still. I wondered what she was dreaming about. I took a seat in the chair next to the window, and for a few minutes, just watched her sleep. It occurred to me that she wore her bracelet even when she slept. What a difference a week can make. Vampires and love, what a tangled web.

I heard a noise down in the kitchen just about than. It was easy to hear since I hadn't been able to get back to sleep.

I walked down the stairs and found Don looking through my fridge.

"Hey Don, what are you doing, making a sandwich?"

"Do you have any steak?"

It was an odd choice for a midnight snack.

"Sorry. We do have Peanut Butter and Jelly."

He leaned against the counter. I poured myself a glass of grape soda.

"Is Vanessa your girlfriend?"

"Oh, no."

"I appreciate you giving me the place to stay. I'm sorry if it's an inconvenience."

"Don't mention it. Hey, are you still going to be able to make court tomorrow?"

"Yeah brother, it's going to be rough but I'll get up in the morning and go."

I turned to walk back upstairs when Don spoke again.

"Brother, she is beautiful. Good luck with that".

"I will need it, thank you."

I was lying down a little while later when I felt a movement on the bed. I sat up and saw Vanessa looking out the window herself.

"Can't sleep?" I asked.

"I guess I'm a little worried about the whole vampire thing."

"Yeah, I am too."

She sat down on the corner of the bed.

"Do you think it's real?"

"I hope not. But Don can be pretty convincing."

I felt her hand touch my leg. I scooted myself next to her on the corner of the bed.

She was wearing the same clothes she had come to my house in. I was meanwhile dressed in a t-shirt and pajamas. We sat on the corner of the bed for about a minute without speaking. I rubbed my eyes a little bit.

"I can't make a good omelet." She said suddenly.

"What?"

"I've been trying this recipe; it's a chicken and spinach omelet. I've tried making it twice and messed it up both times."

"We all have mountains to climb. I can't snap my fingers."

"Really?"

"Nor am I a good at whistling."

I tried to whistle but only a hoarse whisper came out. And than I coughed.

"Were you in love with Ricky?" I said out of nowhere.

The mention of his name seemed to bring a frown to her face. It was maybe still a sensitive subject.

"I think so", she said finally.

It hurt to hear her say that. It was the acknowledgement of their maybe being a better man for her. It hurt the most to think that she probably felt about him the way I felt about her.

"Do you want to get back together with him?"

She hesitated before answering.

"No. Sometimes you can love the person and still feel it's not the right person for you. Ricky is special, the way he carries himself, the way he sees life, it's different than most people. But when I try to talk to him about every day things, it's like we're always on a different page. Some times we would argue, and some times it got kind of crazy."

"Crazy?"

"Yes."

"Like Lifetime movie of the week crazy?"

"I'd say so."

I felt both sympathetic and jealous at the same time. I couldn't help but envy Ricky since he had been with her.

"How about you? " She said turning the subject back to me.

"Have I met my Sara Conner? My soul mate? I'd have to say no."

I thought back to all the girls in my life. It was not an impressive resume.

"I remember the first girl I thought I loved was in Kindergarten. The other kids seemed to only care about finger painting and nap time, but I was completely taken with Catherine. I wasn't the most perceptive kid, but man I thought she was perfect."

"Did you act on it?"

"I couldn't. She liked two other boys instead of me. It was a romantic quadrangle. "

"You mean a square?"

"Right, well she didn't like me very much anyways. One day she let me borrow her colored pencils and her crayons, and I gave them back to her all mixed together in one box. She told the teacher."

"She was a tattle tale."

"I didn't like another girl until Stephanie in the third grade."

"Did you have any better luck with her?"

"No", I said flatly. "I saw the movie Aladdin, and I wanted Stephanie to be my Jasmine. But, it literally would have taken a magic carpet for me to win her over."

"Did you tell her how you felt?"

"I didn't come out and say it directly, but it had to be noticeable. The teacher would count off students and put them into groups by whatever number they were given, so I'd calculate and always make sure that I ended up in her group. And I sat across from her at the lunch table every day, and even gave her my apple sauce since I knew it was her favorite."

"But she never knew you liked her?"

"I'm sure she did. On Valentines Day, I left a card on her desk which was not uncommon since in elementary school everybody gets a Valentines Day card. But mine was special; I tucked a Hershey kiss inside of it. And it's not like a Hershey kiss is that easy to get when you're a third grader. "

"So what happened? "

"I stood by the pencil sharpener, pretending to be sharpening my pencil but really just watching closely as she opened it. And she looked real happy. But the smile had nothing to do with her liking me; she just really liked Hershey kisses."

"Sorry."

"It's nothing to be sorry about. I do truly believe that love is about timing and all the right pieces falling into place. Everything has to be perfect for it to work."

"That's true."

"Can I ask you a question?"

"Ok."

"Do you think I should be sort of egocentric? " I asked.

"Different things work for different people. Girls like a guy who is confident, but they also like intelligence."

"I always thought Spider-man had it wrong. The real lesson is that with great intelligence comes great responsibility."

"Girls like nice guys also."

"Hmmm, the word to use there is seldom."

"It's true though."

"Let's forget about every other girl. Let's say we're doing a case study on you. What do you prefer?"

"I like a little of both."

I felt like I knew so much about her and at the same knew so little.

"Do I at least have the market cornered on guys who have fallen for you in the last week?"

"Yes."

Now I was the one who didn't know whether to laugh or cry. We were at a bridge of some sorts. I was not pushing to take advantage of her being in an emotional state. But what was a guy to do when the girl he liked was suddenly single?

"I never thought I'd be sharing a bed with you."

She laughed. "Was that a pick-up line?"

"Too strong?"

"A little bit on the cheesy side."

"Would you rather I approach you directly or indirectly?"

"Your an over thinker."

"Maybe the world's first over thinking underachiever."

"You're not so bad."

"That kiss downstairs. Was it just a moment of passion?"

"I don't know."

"One thing that's pretty obvious to the both of us is how I feel. I think we just have to come to some sort of conclusion about what you want."

"It's not a big deal."

"It is for me. I don't know if I'm pursuing a friend...or something more."

"What do you want Anthony?"

"Just you I guess."

We sat quietly than, for seemingly an eternity. I began to think about what classic literary character I resembled the most. Who of all the classic failures had gotten so close to the one they loved while never winning them over?

"Do you have protection?"

I turned to Vanessa who had the usual look of curiosity burning from her eyes.

"Sure. I hid some garlic under the bed."

"No, that's not what I mean."

"Oh."

There was another moment of silence. She was being patient with me, which is exactly what I needed. How can I describe the feeling when you expect nothing and get it all? It took a while for me to settle my mind down.

"Let me check."

I leaped towards the desk drawer and grabbed my wallet. I had one left, although it may have been a solid two months old.

"How long do these things last?"

She grabbed it out of my hands.

"It should be alright."

She was very casual about the whole thing, as if she was closing a business deal.

"You really want to do this?" I searched again for clarity.

"I think so."

"We can't be on the fence. You think, or you know?"

She looked away for a second, as if she was confronting the thought for the first time. I was struggling with my natural male instincts and my heart wanting her to show some type of commitment.

"I know", she said a second later.

"Ok. So can we kiss?"

"Do you have chapped lips?"

"What?"

"I like to be funny too."

"It's an overrated commodity, trust me."

"Does the lady always have to initiate the kiss?"

"No, for once I should do that."

I leaned in and kissed her. She had eager lips. My whole body was eager.

I backed off a moment later.

"One thing. We need the right music."

"It can't hurt."

I hopped off the bed and ran to the stereo where I started looking through my albums.

I contemplated putting in O-Town's All or Nothing but my senses got the better of me.

"I'm taking requests."

"Do you have any Usher?"

"I don't. How about All-4-One?"

"You like them?"

"They're pretty much the most underrated R and B group of the nineties."

"How about N Sync?"

"No way, I don't want you thinking about Justin Timberlake."

"What do you recommend?"

"I have an idea."

Once the music was set we both stood for a moment as "We Belong" by Pat Benetar played loudly.

"Nice choice."

"Well it was this or 'Hit Me With Your Best Shot."

"Are you going to take off your clothes?" She asked.

"Alright, I'm going to take off my pants, but don't look at my calves ok?"

"Look who is insecure."

"Insecurities are what give us depth. Now I believe it's you're turn."

She took off her clothes, and it was at that exact moment that Madame Craziel's prophecy popped into my head?

"Is something wrong?" She asked as she noticed a slight frown cross my face.

"Don't think I'm crazy, but have you ever in the moment felt like something wasn't meant to happen?"

"Are you saying that we're about to do something wrong?"

My judgment was putting me a bit of a dilemma. It was only falling in love that could force a man to fulfill a prophecy of impending doom.

"Forget it", I said.

She took off her pants a moment later and I was immediately jealous.

"What the hell? You have stronger calves than me! We have to get all that Ricky out of you."

"Jealous?"

"Not for much longer."

16

I woke up in the morning with a tremendous amount of energy. And a bit of pain in my neck. Vanessa was peacefully sleeping. I crept downstairs and discovered that Don was gone.

I took my time making breakfast. My theory with cooking was quality over quantity. I wasn't quite sure where Vanessa and I stood; I didn't want to presume that she was my girlfriend or anything. But I had been so happy that I couldn't resist doing something for her.

It was nothing special, just waffles and hot chocolate. I did chop some blueberries up for the waffles but it was nothing extravagant. I sneaked back into the room and placed the plate next to her. I gently tapped her and she stirred slightly.

"Vanessa", I said lightly.

Her eyes opened.

"Anthony", she whispered.

She took a moment to adjust her eyes.

"Breakfast is served", I said as I motioned towards the plate.

She sat up and looked about. The curiosity that I saw in her eyes when I first met her was still present and accounted for.

She kissed me on the cheek and than dug into the waffles. I let her eat for a minute before asking how she had slept.

"Like a baby", she answered. "What happened to Don?"

"Off to court he went."

"He is kind of a strange guy."

I was surprised that she had formulated such an opinion of him.

"Why do you say that?"

"I had this weird feeling about him last night."

"Really? What kind of feeling?"

She stopped chewing and took a sip of the hot chocolate.

"I don't know what it was exactly. I just felt kind of weird when he was sitting next to me".

I felt like I would have noticed if Don had been acting weird. I didn't recall him doing or saying anything peculiar. But, I thought I knew what it was.

"Oh, he smells kind of odd. I noticed that too."

She finished up breakfast and than began to gather her things. We still hadn't discussed last night, or what the future held for us. I didn't want to be the one to approach the subject. Besides, I had something else on my mind.

"Hey Vanessa, let me ask you something. Does Ricky still have his track team jersey?"

"Yes, why do you ask?"

"It's just something Don told me. He said the guy who was after him was wearing a track team jersey."

"And you think it was Ricky?"

"I don't know."

"Anthony, what are you saying? Is Ricky dangerous?"

I didn't want to ruin the mood by telling her everything that Don and I suspected.

"We don't know for sure yet."

"Should I stay away from him?"

"You know him better than I do. Has he ever tried to hurt you?"

She didn't hesitate. "Not at all."

"Well, it's up to you".

We walked down the stairs and into the living room.

"Last night was nice", I mentioned casually.

"You have really cheesy taste in music", she answered. "I have to get home. I still have so much packing to do".

"Oh, right".

She had inadvertently surmised our situation. Yes, we may have taken a huge step the night before, but nothing was stopping this girl from moving to California.

I don't know what it was that came over me in the next few moments.

"Maybe last night was a mistake", I heard myself say.

She turned and looked at me. "What?"

"Was it meaningful for you?"

"Of course."

"But what of the future?"

"Why can't you ever be about the moment?"

"The same reason that you're not about the future. It's just how our personalities are."

"I can't figure out everything on the spot Anthony. I'm just getting out of a relationship."

"So last night was just a casual affair for you?"

"Why are you jumping to all these conclusions?"

"I'm sorry, it's my nature."

"I just need some time to think about everything."

"So you won't marry me?"

"You didn't propose."

"But what if I did?"

"Don't. I'm not ready to get married."

"Tell me, am I at least the top of your list of pursuers?"

"What kind of person do you think I am?"

"I'm just trying to figure out what seems to be impossible."

"Your important to me, isn't that enough?"

"But you may be in love with Ricky. I guess I have to know where I stand, and it's hard for me to believe that you love us both."

"If you can hate more than one person at once, why can't you love more than one person at the same time?"

"So what are you saying?"

"I'm sorry; I'm not capable of any real conclusion right now."

I didn't blame her. She only wanted to take life one day at a time.

Meanwhile, I was cursed with a certain romantic ideal about how love worked. It just wasn't the way the actual world worked.

"Can I see you again tonight? I'm going to bake a cake."

"I'll let you know" I said a bit coldly.

She took that in slowly and nodded.

I walked her to the door and watched her leave. It seemed to be a really hot day outside as the sun steamed my arm up a little bit.

"Hey Vanessa", I called.

"Yes?"

"Be careful, alright?"

She just nodded.

After she left, I walked around the house and for some reason found myself doing push-ups.

I was awed by my energy level that morning. It was as if I had become a human Red Bull.

Lou wasn't due back until the next day, so I still had the house to myself. I sat down to try to get some more writing done but as usual nothing was coming to me. I wondered if this writer's block was going to be a permanent disease.

The doorbell rang in the early afternoon.

I closed my notebook and walked to door where I found the same little girl scouts who had sold me the double Oreos. They had the exact same expressions as they had before.

"Hey girls, what can I do for you today?"

The leader, wearing the same uniform as before, stepped forward and gave me a large smile.

"Do you want to buy some candy bars from us?"

"Well, I don't think I can afford it."

She gave a hopelessly sad expression. I really didn't have any money for them this time.

"Did you guys get the Rocky Road?"

"No, Miss Olsen said we had to sell these candy bars to get it".

Miss Olsen sounded like a mean witch.

"Aw geez, I'm sorry about that."

"We can give you a free sample". She said with hope.

"I guess it can't hurt."

I opened the door fully and took a step outside. For an unknown reason I suddenly felt a rush of pain.

"What the hell??" I stepped back inside.

The girl looked stunned as she held the candy bar out in her hand.

"You said H-E-Double hockey sticks!"

"Oh, sorry about that."

What in the world was that pain all about?

I stepped outside again and felt the same pain surge through my arms and this time through my whole body. I suddenly felt like I was trapped in a tanning booth with the heat turned up.

I jumped back inside again. I pulled up my sleeve and looked at arm. It looked worse than sun burn; this must be a third degree burn I thought. But, it couldn't be!

What the hell had happened to me?

"Listen, girls, I'm going to have to take a rain check."

"Should we come back when it rains?"

"No, I'm sorry. Perhaps tomorrow? Actually, try Mr. Drunkemiller across the street. He likes candy allots".

I had no idea whether or not Mr. Drunkenmiller liked candy or vegetables. I just needed the girls to go away so I could figure out why my body was shaking in pain.

Deep breathe after deep breath consumed me.

I closed the door and stumbled into my living room.

The pain started to lesson with the more I moved away from the door.

I ended up in the kitchen putting some ice on my arm.

There had to be a logical explanation to all of this.

I had been perfectly fine until the kids came to the door. Than I opened the door and stepped outside and...

Oh no! I suddenly realized what it was. It seemed that walking outside in the sunshine had burned my arm.

Regular sunlight burning somebody was a symptom of something alright. But I wasn't ready to believe it.

It couldn't be what I thought it was.

I quickly threw open the cabinet. I searched through all the spices. Oregano, Cinnamon, where is it? There! Garlic!

I grabbed the Garlic bottle and felt my hands go numb and the air in my lungs go away.

"Ohhhhhhhhhh shiiiiiiiiiiiit", my voice carried as my throat felt like it was on fire.

I dropped the bottle immediately and staggered towards the sink where I turned on the fosset and let cold water pour into my mouth.

"Oh shit", I muttered again as I limped to the couch in my living room.

I took a seat on the couch and tried to recollect my thoughts.

It had been the kind of pain I hadn't felt since I broke my ankle back in the eighth grade while playing basketball.

At this point, the evidence all pointed to one impossible conclusion.

Somehow, someway, I had made the transformation over night.

I had become a vampire.

17

Mr. Ryan must have noticed all the sun tan lotion I had spread on my face because he was looking at me as if I was a weirdo. I took a seat in my normal spot and scratched myself. I had remembered that I had a scheduled meeting with him and I didn't want to miss it or else my uncle would have heard and gotten angry. Man, why was I itching so much?

"Anthony, how have you been?"

"A bit thirsty."

"Would you like a cup of water?"

"No, I don't think that would quite do it for me at this point."

"How is the girl situation?"

"There have been some developments."

"Did you steal her from the boyfriend?"

"Not exactly how it went down, no."

"You seem a little bit different today Anthony."

He scratched his chin. I tried to play it cool.

"I flossed this morning."

"So we've had three sessions, do you feel like you've been making progress?"

"Oh yeah, absolutely. Man is it hot in here or is it just me?"

"I'm sorry; I must have turned the air condition off."

I toyed with the idea of telling Mr. Ryan about what had happened to me. I genuinely wanted advice.

"Listen, um, have you ever gone through serious changes as an adult?"

"Anthony, I know exactly what you're talking about."

"You do?"

"Yes. You're going through something called resocialization. It's when we change our behavior as adults in order to eliminate bad habits."

"Oh, right. Well actually, my changes are more in the physical realm."

He batted an eye.

"Anything specific you want to tell me Anthony?"

I tried to gauge how crazy my confession would sound to an outside observer.

"Not at the moment."

"Well I'll be here when you're ready. Have you given any more thought to graduate school?"

"Yeah, I have."

"And?"

"I think I want to go. And honestly I have to thank you because I was really out of it when we first started talking. But I feel like I've conquered my demons and I'm ready to be a functioning member of society."

"I'm glad to hear that Anthony. "

"One question I have though."

"Yes?"

"Do graduate schools have night classes?"

Nobody dreams about growing up and becoming a vampire. It's just not on your average list of things an adult does. How can a vampire make a living anyways? He can really only do overnight jobs since he can't be out in the sun. I guess I would have to become a fan of Denny's and IHOP.

These were the stupid thoughts that were going through my head as I paced around my room. And there was one gigantic question looming. Did this mean I would have to attack people and drink their blood?

I turned the television on and flipped it to Dr. Phil's show. There was a mother who was having problems with her daughter growing apart from her. Then I switched over to Tyra who was giving advice to obese women on how to have more self confidence and how to see their inner beauty.

But none of the talk shows seemed to be talking about what to do if you become a vampire.

I rang Robert and told him that it was an emergency and that I needed him to drop everything he was doing and come over immediately.

He arrived about thirty five minutes later. As it turns out, the frozen pizza he had put in the oven was such a priority that he had waited until it was done and ate it before coming over.

"Alright man, I'm here. What the hell is going on?"

I didn't know how to say it.

"Something weird is happening to me. It's hard to explain."

He eyed me suspiciously for a moment.

"Wait, you're not coming out of the closet or anything right?"

"What? No, nothing like that."

"I'm listening."

I took a deep breathe.

"I'm a vampire".

Robert didn't respond at first. It took a moment for it to set in for him.

"Awesome!"

"What?"

"Where have you been? Being a vampire is totally in style. I'm tellin you Anthony, they get all the women!"

"Ok. But what about the fact that if I go out in the sunlight my skin burns. And if i'm around garlic it feels like I'm choking. Do you know how hard its going to be avoid garlic when I work at a pizza place??"

"I admit, there are some drawbacks."

"It's crazy man. Do you remember what Madame Craziel told me? She said I would have a moment of true love and than I would die. Well Vanessa stayed over last night, and now I'm one of the undead! It was spot on!"

"So what happened last night?"

"Without going into details, it was a nice night"

"Man. I've heard about guys getting girls pregnant or getting STD's. Now on top of that you have to worry about becoming a vampire!"

He started to pace around the room. I was nervous but Robert seemed to be even more so,

"What are you so wired up about?" I asked.

"It's not every day your best friend tells you he's a vampire. Are you going to slaughter people now or what?"

"It is not an issue I want to think about but I guess I have to confront it sooner or later. From everything I know, vampires need to drink blood in order to survive. How else can I live?"

"Maybe it tastes like Sunny Delight?"

"Somehow I doubt that. What am I going to do?"

We both were panicked but now was the time to brainstorm and come up with a solution.

"There is only one way to make you human again."

I thought back to my horror movie knowledge.

"Yes! I just have to kill the vampire who turned me!"

"That's right. You have to kill whoever it was that came into your house last night and bit you".

"So that's Ricky than right?"

Robert sighed. He had already thought of something that again maybe I didn't want to confront.

"You say that Vanessa was sleeping in your room last night right?"

I put my hands up.

"You can't honestly be thinking that?"

"We have to consider every possibility here. She was there in the room with you, who's to say she didn't bite you?"

"She wouldn't do that."

"What? C'mon man! She could easily be a vampire."

"If she is than I'll make it work. If anything it makes her and I more compatible if we're both vampires."

"Hello Mcfly! What about the part where vampires go around killing people and drinking blood? You don't want to do that".

He was right. Vampires were dangerous creatures. I was a dangerous creature.

"But if Vanessa was a vampire, than whom was it attacking us in the cemetery and chasing us?"

Robert chewed on that for a moment.

"What if Vanessa and Ricky are a vampire couple? Maybe he's the original vampire and than he turned her?"

"Than I wouldn't really know which one bit me. It could have been Ricky."

"You may need to kill them both."

My head hurt. I had the type of headache that I didn't suppose Advil would cure.

"I would never kill or attempt to kill Vanessa unless I knew for one hundred percent that she was a vampire."

"Then we have to find out."

"I'm going to hang here. But when the sun does down I'm going to pay a little visit to Madame Craziel and find out what she really knows. Listen, Robert. No matter what happens, I want you to know that I would never try to kill you or drink your blood."

"Gee, thanks buddy."

As soon as it got dark I was on my way back to the carnival. It was a lot less crowded this time. I guess people could only ride the Ferris wheel so many times before it became boring.

I paid the entrance fee and than started to make my way through the bright lights of the carnival. A sudden craving hit my stomach, and it wasn't for Honey Comb.

"Oh geez", I muttered to myself as I desperately searched for the tent.

The thirst, it was making my heart pound fast and the sweat drip from me like I was in a sauna.

I stopped at a vendor and ordered a drink. My throat felt so incredibly raw and parched, I wanted anything to help it out.

I paid the four dollars and took a huge sip of the drink.

And spit it out immediately.

Even though Grant Hill drank Sprite, for a vampire it did nothing but burn my tongue.

I was fresh out of luck. My body was calling for blood.

I was almost limping than, drawing the attention of people who didn't know what to make of my animalistic behavior.

I felt pain all through out my body. In my mouth, I felt the famous vampire fangs taking form.

All of this blood sitting around, just waiting to be taken. It could easily be mine, I told myself.

It was seeing the tent that made me temporarily take my mind off the thirst.

I was nearly crawling by the time I entered through the black drapes.

Madame Craziel was sitting at her table with her cat pebbles. They had been having a jolly good time until they saw me slither in.

"Young man, you do not look healthy." She said as she popped some tropical skittles into her mouth.

I felt a sudden surge of aggressiveness enter me.

"Well, you look old."

"Honey, I am old."

"You can also be dead."

"What?"

"Oh what, you don't know? I'm a vampire!! And it's because of you!"

"You mean my prophecy came true?"

"That's right Nostradamus. The world may not end in 2012, but Anthony Hasher surely has become one of the undead."

I felt them now for sure. The fangs were hanging outside of my mouth. I opened up wide and showed them to Madame. She gasped. I don't know why she was so surprised, it had been her prophecy.

"Is this some type of joke?" She asked.

"No, I'm actually in the process of contemplating whether or not to stick these fangs in your throat."

I made a move towards her and she quickly picked up a cup of water and threw it on me.

I stood for a moment and than wiped the water from my eyes.

"Madame, I think what you're looking for is holy water. You just threw regular old Aquafina on me."

"Oh, damn", she said as I moved in on her.

I grabbed her by the throat and looked down at her neck.

The anticipation of blood was making my spine tingle.

My fangs were watering up; my whole body was feeling a rush!

"Wait", Madamme cried.

I stopped for a moment and looked at her.

"Let me guess. You're going to offer me a full refund?"

"No, but I can help you with your situation."

"Oh? Do tell."

"Give me your hand. I will give you a new prophecy."

I backed up for a moment.

"Do you think your mumbo jumbo will work on a vampire?"

"Yes", she said simply.

I took a deep breathe and took a seat next to her. If I sucked her blood, I'd feel great. But that wasn't the reason I had come. I had to come to get more information from her.

"You're lucky that I'm half vampire, half nice guy. Plus I'm desperate."

She took my hand and worked her magic.

It only took a moment for her head to start spinning like the exorcist.

"Wow!!" She said when her eyes opened.

"What is it?"

"There is so much pain in the prophecy."

"Just for once can't I be given something hopeful?"

"I saw the one that you love."

"Vanessa?"

"She is in grave danger! You must go to her immediately!"

"What's going to happen to her?"

"Only you can save her, but you must go now!"

"Right!"

I jumped up from the chair and ran out of the tent.

It occurred to me that the Madame could easily have been telling me a lie simply to save her own life.

But I didn't care. Something about being a vampire brought out the emotional instability in me.

I ran through the carnival and made it back to my car two minutes later.

There was another envelope sitting on the hood.

I pulled it off the hood and ripped it open.

"Oh no", I said as I had read the content.

"Tonight, she is MINE"!

I saw Robert's car parked across the street from Ricky's House so I pulled up right behind him.

He got out of his car and I saw a huge wooden stake in his hand.

"Where in the world did you get that?"

"I found it my backyard. Dad is quite the lumberjack actually."

"So I have to put that through his heart?"

He nodded as we both looked at the house across the street.

"And what happened to Buffy the Vampire slayer?"

Robert sighed. "She wanted to do movies."

"Where is Don?" I asked.

"He should be here soon."

We started to walk across the street, taking painfully slow footsteps.

Every step brought us closer to a final destination.

We stepped onto the sidewalk, right next to Ricky's mailbox.

"Are you scared?" Robert asked.

"One benefit to being a vampire is that I don't get scared. I have the endurance of Kobe Bryant and the thirst of a dehydrated guy lost in the dessert, but no apparent fear."

"So what exactly is the plan here?" Robert asked as he handed me the stake.

I took control of the stake which was neither heavy nor light. It felt very natural having it in my hand.

"I guess I have to sneak up to his room and put this through is heart."

"But what if he's not home?"

"We have to take our chances."

A hand grabbed me and I turned around with the stake raised above my head.

"What in the world?"

It was Don, standing with a giant smile.

"Hey buddy, do you mind pointing that stake in the other direction?"

"Don, where did you come from?"

"My house."

"I'm glad your here. We need you to positively identify him before I stake him."

"Are you guys sure this is a smooth idea. I mean if he sees us coming, he's going to kill all of us".

Robert pulled out a cross and some garlic.

"Whoa", Don said, "make sure you keep that stuff away from Anthony.

We don't want to accidentally do him in."

"Alright, I think we should split up."

"That is stupid", Robert complained. "That happens in every horror movie, and somebody always ends up dead."

"Yeah but we can't all go strolling into his room. That will make too much noise."

"How about this", Don offered. "Why don't you go in through the front Anthony and I'll go in through the back. And Robert can stay here just in case somebody comes home."

"I'll wait by my car", Robert chimed in.

"Alright, when you get in the house Don, I want you to stand guard downstairs while I go up to his room. I'm going to sprinkle some garlic on him like we planned and see how he reacts. Robert, if you see anything coming I want you to text my phone, alright?"

"Sounds like a plan."

Robert handed me a pinch of garlic.

 Hey Don, do you want some of this?"

Don shook his head. "I brought holy water brother."

"You had it blessed by a priest?"

"The old man's profession finally paid off."

"I think we're ready to do this".

We all looked at each other but nobody made a move. This was all because of me in a way so I took the first step. I walked through the front yard and right to the front porch. To the right of me I saw Don creeping into the backyard towards the back door. I looked back at Robert who was leaning against his car with his keys shuffling in his hand.

Ricky's house looked very plain and average. I guess I was expecting an established vampire to have his own apartment, or maybe a castle. There were three flower pots next to the front door, all freshly watered. A big rocking chair sat on the edge of the porch, moving slowly back and forth,

It was put up or shut up time. I reached for the doorknob slowly. I had to be extremely careful not to make more than slight noise. When my hand was on the doorknob I turned it clockwise and heard a click. It was definitely unlocked. I let me hand rotate the knob as the door began to slowly creak open.

Terrible darkness. What did I expect from a house at night? It was pitch black as I took a step inside. All that I had to see was coming from the light outside, but I knew I had to close the door behind me. I gently pushed it until it was closed; it made a small screeching noise before closing. I walked through the living room searching for signs of anything that would indicate a vampire lived there.

There was a picture in the living room of Ricky standing with his track team. Above that was a family portrait of Ricky and his parents. I admired the picture of Ricky holding a trophy after winning a track meet. I remembered being in the stands for that one. High school was so long ago.

I heard a tiny noise in the distance and quickly looked up from the pictures. It may have been Don finally getting into the through the back door. If the interior of this house was like mine then that would put Don right in the kitchen. I couldn't quite call out his name however.

I grasped the stake firmly and made my way towards the staircase. So far, I had heard no rumblings from upstairs, not even a stir. My biggest fear was that Ricky's parents were home. If they were awake and found me than it would a very hard situation to explain. I couldn't very well tell Ricky's mom that her son was a vampire that I had come to vanish from existence.

The staircase was average in length, but it seemed like forever before I got to the top stair. There was one hallway upstairs, with two bedrooms to the left of me and one bedroom down at the other end. In my house, my room was the one on the far right. If Ricky liked to have his privacy he would have made sure that he too had the room by itself at the end of the hallway. So I turned in that direction and continued to walk at a slow pace.

I thought of every horror movie I had ever seen. I didn't think I had broken any rules or made any of the decisions that characters usually make. We all had jointly come to the decision that I needed to kill the vampire, to save myself, and to save the town from future vampire slayings.

Plus, Madame Craziel had said that Vanessa was in immediate danger, and it made sense. You break up with your boyfriend who happens to be a vampire and there is a good chance he might come back looking for trouble.

I was two steps away from the bedroom when I froze for a moment.

What if he is awake?

I would have to fight him.

Could I take him?

I had vampire strength now. And with that came a certain swagger and confidence. But for all I knew, more experienced vampires may have even more strength than rookies. And I'm sure he knew some tricks that I hadn't discovered yet.

But I had to put all those doubts out of my mind. It was him or me.

I saw that the door to his room was closed. I put my hand on the knob and opened it slowly. I maybe should have just swung it open quickly, using the element of surprise. But for some unknown reason, I took the slow and direct approach. The light in his room was off which meant there was a good possibility that he wasn't home.

I walked a few steps into the room and again looked for any signs that it was a vampire living there. Again, I saw more track team memorabilia and even a yearbook from high school. To the left of me there were insurance papers sitting on the ground. I remember thinking that Ricky really wasn't a bad guy after that day he had come to my house. That was key however, because it was that day that I invited him into my house. A vampire needs an invitation to enter, but once he gets it he is forever welcome.

I was standing in the middle of the room when the bed caught my attention. The white sheets of course stood out in the dark. And there seemed to be something in the sheets.

I walked to the bed and looked down. There was definitely something in the bed.

A big part of me urged me to get out of the house right now. But I had to know what was under the sheet.

I held the stake in a striking position. .

This time I went with the element of surprise. I reached forward quickly and pulled the sheet up.

"Ohhhhhhhhhhhhh", I cried out as I put my hand to my mouth.

The stake dropped out of my hand.

It was a body.

Ricky's body.

I wondered if a vampire could puke or not.

Ricky's throat had been ripped out. He was laying there with his eyes open, staring at the ceiling. I could only guess that somebody had attacked him while he was sleeping, making quick work of him.

I was breathing hard, even as the undead I still reacted as any human would.

I gingerly placed the sheet back over his body and picked up the stake from the ground. Then I made my way back down the stairs. This time I wasn't as concerned with how much noise I made. Ricky's parents didn't seem to be home.

As soon as the front door closed behind me I jumped off the porch and ran across the street where I saw Robert standing there anxiously.

"What happened man?"

I put the stake in the back seat of the car and looked at Robert.

"He's up there."

"You killed him?"

"No, he was already dead when I got there. His throat had been torn up just like Becky's."

"So he isn't the vampire than."

I glanced around.

"What the hell happened to Don?"

"He didn't come out of the house", Robert said. "I was hoping he was with you. Do you think he's alright?"

"Let's go to the back and see if he's there."

We crept back through the front yard. I would have been more comfortable hopping in the car and driving as far away as possible but we had to know if Don was alright. Where the hell was he?

Ricky had a backyard that was big enough to run laps, which I'm sure he had done many times. Robert and I tiptoed past the water hose and towards the back deck.

"Should I call out his name?" Robert asked

"No, the killer could still be around. Let's be as quiet as possible."

"OH NO!"

I saw Robert looking past me. I turned around and gasped.

Don.

He was hanging off the deck, a rope around his neck.

Robert didn't have the benefit of being a vampire and so he turned and threw up.

"What the hell?" I cried.

"I'm going to be sick", Robert was saying.

Don's body continued swinging from side to side.

I thought about going to make sure he was gone but it was pretty obvious. I don't believe my stomach would have been able to handle it anyways.

After a few minutes we made our way back to the car.

"What now?" Robert asked.

"I really thought it was Ricky."

I leaned against the car, unsure of how to proceed.

"Hey, do you have the article that you found in the library?"

"Yeah, it's in the car."

I sat in the front seat of the car and unfolded the article.

Surely enough, the story was very close to what Robert had told

Heather and me. A guy and a girl in a house, and the police barge in and shoot the guy. No word on what happened to Doug; only that he was the prime suspect in the murders.

I flipped to the second page where they actually had a picture of the girl.

It caught my attention immediately as it always did.

The shining glow, elegant but not expensive.

The girl in the picture was wearing Vanessa's bracelet

"Oh no", I said out loud.

Robert climbed into the passenger seat.

"What is it?"

"I just found out who the girl in the story is".

"Who?"

"Vanessa's grandmother."

"It's eleven twenty. The anniversary ends in forty minutes. We have to get to her house right now. "

"Are we going to take the vampire out ourselves?" Robert asked.

"We have no choice. We saw what happened the last time the police got involved."

"We need a backup plan. Listen, I'll meet you at Vanessa's house."

He started to move towards his car. I grabbed him by the shoulder.

"What? There's no time."

He wrestled my shoulder off and looked me dead in the eye.

"Trust me, we may need reinforcements. I'll be there soon."

I let him go, watching him drive off. Maybe he did have a backup plan. I didn't know whether to believe him or not. I guess I couldn't blame him if he was bailing on me. This was never his battle and he was only risking his life by coming with me.

I didn't have time to think about it. It was all about getting to Vanessa's house now.

I drove about ten miles over the speed limit as I zig zagged through the town's back streets.

It was going to be me or him, I kept telling myself. There were no other options left.

But who the hell was the vampire?

My car clock read eleven thirty four when I pulled up to Vanessa's house.

There were no cars parked outside of Vanessa's house.

I exited my car and jogged across the street.

"She is in grave danger", Madame Craziel's latest warning played back in my head.

I stumbled through her grass and felt the thirst beginning to consume me again.

It was more painful than ever, causing me to collapse to the ground and look up at the stars.

The stars were blurry but I could have sworn to seen fate and destiny take shape. They were two big people standing in the sky. And they were laughing at me.

"Sons of bitches", I muttered.

I slowly got to my knees and started crawling towards the front porch.

My hand reached for the doorknob and I used it to drag myself to my feet.

I rung the doorbell and leaned my face against the door. I felt sweat running down my forehead.

The door opened and Vanessa appeared, looking a bit spooked by my appearance.

"Anthony, I didn't think you were coming over tonight."

"Can I come in?" I asked while turning to look behind me.

"Sure." She opened the door and I floated inside.

I went straight to the kitchen, than back to the living room. I felt a little better only after I had given the entire first floor a look around.

"Is everything alright?" Vanessa seemed confused by my anxiousness.

"Did anybody come by here?" I asked.

"No, why do you ask?"

"I'll tell you in a minute. Do me a favor and lock the front door, and I'll go lock the back."

"Why?"

"There is no time! Just do it!"

She walked away towards the front door while I took care of the back. We met back in the living room a moment later.

"Vanessa, I have to ask you something incredibly important. Outside of me, have you met any new guys in the last few weeks?"

"No."

I nodded slowly and than took a seat on the couch. She sat next to me.

"What the hell is going on Anthony? Why did you bring a stake into my house?"

I took a few breaths before speaking.

"Everything Don told you about the vampire is true. We thought it was Ricky, but it's somebody else."

A look of fear came into Vanessa's eyes as she stood from the couch.

"Is the Vampire after us?"

"Yes, well no, he's after you actually."

"Why me?

"I can't explain the whole story right now; I just know that there is a good chance he's going to come after you in the next twenty minutes".

Vanessa looked around her own house cautiously. I was trying to remain calm on the couch while the seconds ticked away in my mind.

"How did the cake go?"

"What?"

"You were going to bake a cake right?"

"Yes, it came out nicely."

"I'm glad to hear that."

There was nothing like small talk to kill the time.

Only fifteen minutes left.

"I would love to have a slice of your cake in about twenty minutes". I said nervously.

Vanessa was standing, holding tightly to her bracelet. I noted that it was something she did whenever she was in trouble. It was like the bracelet was a protector, keeping her from harm.

Screeeeeeeeeeeeeeee

My ears picked it up immediately. My vampire senses were mightily heightened.

"Did you hear that?"

Vanessa listened very closely but she couldn't hear the noise.

Screeeeeeeeeeeeeeee

"Sounds like a door closing. It's coming from upstairs."

Vanessa gulped as I stood from the couch. She grabbed my arm.

"Don't go up there!"

"It's probably nothing", I said lying.

"This is where you seeing so many horror movies should pay dividends. It's always something!"

I took her hand off my arm.

"The only thing I can do to protect you is to stop him".

She stood than, shoulder to shoulder with me. Her eyes were searching for something as she looked me up and down.

"Why do you have to protect me?"

I could suddenly relate to Doug. He had confessed his love all those years ago, only to have the police come in and ruin it. There was always something standing in the way of true love.

I peered back at the clock. It was ten minutes to midnight. When I looked back at Vanessa, her eyes hadn't let up. I put my hand on her shoulder.

"I'm sorry the way I acted this morning."

She grabbed my hand. It didn't seem like she was accepting my answer.

"That's it?"

I looked down at my shoes. They were rusty and exhausted, just like I was mentally. I looked up at her again, this time with absolute clarity.

"That pretty much is it."

"I could be dead in fifteen minutes."

I nodded.

"Alright, listen, this is hard for me to say. In fact, I've never actually told a woman this."

"Yes?"

"I have strong feelings for you"

"That's not the right way to say it."

"Ok, if there is such a thing as love in its truest form than that is how I feel about you. Are you happy?"

She smiled. We could have lived happily ever after if it wasn't for the fact that a vampire was after us. There was also the small detail I had left out about me having become one.

"I believe this is where you say you also love me?"

She hesitated.

"I suppose I do."

"That is a very half empty answer. If we get out of this I am expecting something a bit more solid!"

"Ok just be careful."

"And if we make it, can you bake me some brownies?"

She was a little caught off guard by my off beat suggestion but she managed a smile that for my heart was priceless.

"Sure."

"If you never invited this guy inside than there is no way he can be here."

I walked towards the stairs with the stake in my hand gain. There was now eight minutes left until midnight.

I made my way up the stairs. There had been enough suspense and fear for one night at Ricky's house, and now I was going through a similar situation again.

When I was at the top of the stairs I listened closely for the noise again.

I began to look through each room. Time was on my side, three minutes until midnight.

It was when I got to the last room that I tensed up a bit. Be strong, I warned myself.

I didn't find anything in the last room so I walked back into the hallway.

It was there on the top of the stairs that I looked at my watch and saw destiny.

It was midnight.

But he had never been invited, so how could be here anyways?

A thought started to enter my mind as I looked down the stairs and saw Vanessa on the couch.

The article from the library, there was something about it that I had missed.

What was it?

My eyes grew wide at what it was.

"Hey Vanessa", I called.

"Are you ok?" She yelled back.

"Yes. I have to ask you something. Whose house is this?"

"What do you mean?"

"How did this house come into your family?"

She had to think about it for a second. Her answer came a few seconds later.

"It was my grandmothers."

I stood, frozen. So the vampire had always had an invitation. He got it forty years ago.

"Boo", I heard from behind me.

I saw out of the corner of my eye that somebody was standing there behind me with what looked to be a sledgehammer in his hand.

I made a quick turn with the stake, as quick my as vampire abilities would allow me. But I was too late. Maybe if I could have been a track star in high school and than combined that with vampire abilities I could have been quick enough. But I was just an average guy who had become a vampire, and this guy had at least forty years of vampirism under his belt.

So the stake merely hit air as the sledgehammer pummeled me in the stomach.

I yelled as best as I could while having the wind knocked out of me.

When I looked up I saw him winding up with the sledgehammer again.

I didn't know if I could handle another hit. But, there wasn't much choice given to me.

He swung, hard and fast, catching me right in the side of the head.

I fell backwards, down the stairs, crumbling in agony until I landed at the very bottom.

There was so much pain, a little bit too much considering that I was a vampire. The pain was familiar. I quickly surmised that the vampire had spread garlic on the tip of the sledgehammer.   He had withstood the pain himself in order to hurt me.

Vanessa stood on top of me, scared out of her wits. I tried to lift my hand and say something, I wanted to tell her to get out, but the wind was really gone from me and I couldn't speak.

And than came the darkness. Everything started to get dark and I thought I heard a familiar laugh before I went numb and than unconscious.

21

I awoke a few moments later to find myself tied up in a chair with a slice of garlic bread sitting on the floor in front of me. And the vampire laughing at me.

Don Cramers, laughing at me.

That brings you to my where I'm at currently. Don is now sitting on the couch with Vanessa. She isn't tied up but she's too afraid to try to run away. And with good reason, Don has us both at his mercy.

"You're so thick Anthony. I can't believe you didn't figure it out earlier."

He speaks differently now. The surfer boy lingo has completely disappeared. I guess it was just apart of the disguise.

The garlic is making every breath hard. But I manage to squeak out, "I thought we were friends.:

Don laughs again, and than pulls out an apple which he takes a bite out of.

"Don't be surprised Anthony. I've developed quite the taste for these foods over the years. And you would too if you were going to be living past the next few minutes."

"I thought we were friends", I repeated.

" Fool! We were never friends. You have been a thorn in my side. You've been around Vanessa a bit too much recently for my liking. You and Ricky, but I took care of him already. Once I brutally gorify you, there will be nothing left to stand between me and my bride to be."

"I don't want to be your wife Don", Vanessa says firmly but Don can only laugh again.

"It's your choice. You can be with me like your grandmother wanted to, or I can kill you."

"What are you talking about?" Vanessa asks.

"Silly girl. Didn't Anthony here tell you about you're history? Your grandmother was my first love forty years ago. I wanted her to be like me, to travel the world with me and live the type of life that a stupid human would never be able to provide her. But the police had other plans. They shot me, many times. They didn't count on me surviving. When I got out of the hospital you're grandmother was gone. Her parents had taken her away somewhere. When I tracked her down, she had already died."

"I don't believe you."

"Oh really? Your boyfriend here has an article about it."

Vanessa looks at me and I nod. She doesn't know what to think. I feel like I'm dying.

"This house remained, and I stayed around this town for forty years, waiting for some hope. I created new identities, went to high school more than a few times, and just for kicks I even told my story to classmates and turned it into a town legend. When your mom divorced your dad she moved back here. She was too old for my liking, but I knew she must have a daughter somewhere, I could sense it. So I didn't reveal myself, I instead waited for you.

My eyes are getting dizzy. I don't know how much more I can take. It's usually a good thing when the bad guy starts telling his story, but in this case more time means more pain.

"I sensed when you had moved here. I followed the smell and I saw you one night outside of your house, getting the mail. I saw you wearing the bracelet. You're grandmother loved that bracelet; she never left home without it. And you're the same way."

"Yes", Vanessa says looking down on it. "It's everything to me."

"Do you know where she got it? I gave it to her."

"No!" Vanessa cries

"It is true", Don says while holding her hand. "It's symbolic of how the humans tried to keep me away from your grandmother. She loved me, just as you will."

Don puts his hand up to Vanessa's face and somehow starts to move it back and forth.

Vanessa falls into a trance and suddenly stops blinking. She stares straight ahead, lifeless. The bastard has possessed her.

"Heyyy", I say with a slurred voice. "Enough of this Dracula crap. You get out of here or there is going to be trouble!"

Don lets go of her hands and looks directly at me.

"Anthony, I'm truly sorry you had to be involved in all of this. I never meant to turn you into a vampire. I wasn't going to kill you in the cemetery, just scare you away from Vanessa. I stole Ricky's car so that you would think it was him. And of course you did.

But when I saw how Vanessa felt about you, I had to turn you. I wanted you to tell her that you were a vampire, and I wanted her to still care about you. I wanted her to feel like she could love a vampire. But, you never told her did you? Well, if it makes you feel better, there was a time when I liked you enough to consider letting you live. It was a very short moment, but it did take place. But than, you had to go and ruin my anniversary didn't you? What did you think? That I was going to parish into dust once the clock struck midnight? Are you that stupid?"

"Maybe", is all I can muster as I start to feel the darkness again.

Don stands up and grabs the stake from the couch.

"Now I'm going to have to put you out of your misery. And than I'm going to turn you're girlfriend here into a vampire and we are going to rule this planet."

He walks towards me with the stake. I'm powerless to defend myself. This is it for me.

Than I hear the crash.

I look up with one eye and see Robert! He had run into the room and tackled Don to the ground. But now Don is up on his feet, and he looks angry. Robert looks at me and than backs up. Don is coming right after him but Robert pulls a cross out of his pocket and holds it towards Don.

"Be gone from this world Demon!" Robert screams.

Don looks at him suspiciously for a second and than gives a hearty laugh.

"Stupid idiot! You have to have faith for that cross to work on me."

Don smacks the cross out of his hands and than picks up Robert high in the air.

"I feel stupider for having met you. And because of that, I'm going to have hurt you bad!"

He launches Robert across the room. I hear a thud as Robert bounces off the wall.

A hand grabs my arms and starts to untie the ropes that bind me.

I turn and with my other eye see Heather untying me.

"Whoa", I mutter. "You must be the reinforcements."

She gives half a smile. "Shut up Anthony. I'm getting you out of here."

She unties me pretty quick.

"So what's new with you?"

"I got into medical school."

"Your first choice?"

"Second actually."

"Congratulations!"

"Maybe we should talk later."

"Oh, right."

I point out the garlic bread to her and tell her to 'get it away from me.

Than I tell her to get out of the proximity. I don't want her to be in danger.

I have to get to Robert before Don kills him. I look across the room and see that Don is pounding away on Robert. He has a bloody nose now and his eyes are starting to roll into the back of his heads.

"Don!" I scream. He turns and sees me and let's Robert go.

"You sadistic son of a bitch! This is between you and me!"

He looks at me bitterly and gives an evil nod. He than starts to run towards me. I have no choice but to run back at him.

We meet halfway; at least my face meets with his fist.

I fall to the ground in pain. But I jump back to my feet quickly.

"I'm going to enjoy this", Don cries as he throws another first.

I duck however, and catch him with an elbow right to his stomach.

I look up and see a kind of shocked look on his face. He probably hasn't felt pain in forty years.

"How did you do that?" He asks as I stand up.

"It was a big mistake turning me into a vampire." I say simply as I wind up and throw a hard left hook. It catches him in the jaw and he staggers backwards. He falls right next to the garlic sprinkled sledgehammer. He grins when he feels it in his elbow.

"I'm going to take great pleasure in destroying you." He picks up the sledgehammer. I can see him wincing with the garlic so close.

I brace myself for a beating.

He catches me in the leg on his first swing. I hadn't expected a low shot. The strategy pays off because when I reach for my leg he catches me totally by surprise with the second swing that gets me in the shoulder. I fall to my knees, hopelessly in pain.

He stands before me, with the sledgehammer high above his head.

"Finally, I can get rid of this annoyance. Don't worry about Vanessa, I'm going to feed her with you're blood."

It's the second time that night that I'm looking death right in the eyes.

He winds the hammer back.

"Hey Vanessa, watch this." He says, but than he freezes. He peers beyond me over at the couch, expecting to see Vanessa. But, she isn't there.

"What? Where did she go?"

I see her than, no longer in a trace. She is standing behind him with the stake in her hands.

"She's closer than you think", I say with a bloody smile.

"It can't be", he says before turning around.

A loud, intense scream penetrates the room as Vanessa plunges the stake into Don's heart.

Thankfully, a bit of his blood lands on my forehead. It drips down into my mouth. Ahhh, it tastes like a bottle of Gatorade after a two on two basketball game.

Don falls to his knees, staring back and forth between Vanessa and me.

The shock on his face evokes a bit of sympathy in me.

Don Cramers was an evil vampire, but once upon a time he was just somebody who encountered the same problems we all do. For him, it had all started because he had loved a girl. Who know if he had bad intentions before they took away the love of his life? As it is with many of us, the world didn't allow them to be together.

He dies a moment later. He doesn't descinigrate into ashes like I've seen in movies. He just falls silent and stops moving. In the end it seemed that he died like any human would. We will have to get rid of the body.

I see Robert stirring a little bit over in the corner. He is badly beaten up, but I think he's going to be alright.

My body feels a little bit better after the taste of Don's blood.

My attention turns to Vanessa. She drops the stake and stumbles back against the wall. She came out of the trance just at the right moment. I don't think to ask her what it was that made her come and save my life. I just chalk it up to one of those special moments in life that on the surface seem unexplainable.

I stand and move towards her.

We stand by the wall for a moment.

"How about those brownies?" She says.

22

I quit my job at Pizza Village the next day. Spinning pizza just doesn't seem important anymore. After that I make an appearance in court where I present the owner of Video Club a new copy of Mr. Holland's Opus.

I spend the rest of the day with Vanessa. We travel to her favorite steak place in town.

"Why did you bring me here?" I asked.

"We played basketball, my thing is steak."

"Steak is your sanctuary huh?"

"I guess it is."

She grabbed my hand. "Can you repeat what you said yesterday?"

"Why do you always want me to say it? In public no less?"

"You don't have to say it. I know how you feel."

"Women always want to hear it though."

"I'm actually very satisfied with your level of emotional expression".

"Thank you."

"Are you coming over tonight?"

"Yes. I'm going to help you conquer that crazy omelet."

She laughs. "If you say so."

"Have you finished packing?"

"Not quite. Anthony, do you think California is too far?"

"It's not as far as you might think."

"But it's expensive getting there."

"Oh I wouldn't say that. It all depends on your means of travel."

"I thought about what you said, you know, the morning after."

"It's alright. I understand now is not the time for you to be making the big commitment. Your going to need time. And that I have a lot of."

"I'm glad you understand."

I stare at the table next to us and see a kid sitting in front of a birthday cake. He has a wide smile on his face as he makes a wish and blows out the candle.

Vanessa interrupts my thoughts. "You're going to come and visit as soon as possible right?"

"I've been meaning to tell you something."

"You're not going to visit?"

"Sure, but there is something else you have to know."

The waitress brings our food over. I look at the steak on the plate in front of me and than look back up at the waitress.

"Did you make sure it's extra bloody?"

Robert is released from the hospital two weeks later. He is recovering nicely from a concussion and a broken arm. I meet up with him outside of the hospital and am surprised to find Heather there waiting also.

"Heather, I never got to thank you for helping out that night. You were a life saver."

"No problem", she says as we see Robert coming towards the entrance way.

He gives her a hug. He than throws me a high five.

"You see what kind of friend I am? I took a beating for you!"

"I appreciate it sir."

We're walking back towards the parking lot when Robert asks me about that night. I tell him everything that happened. We get to the cars and Heather steps in the driver side. Robert begins to get an odd look on his face.

"Anthony, there is one thing that I don't understand about what you just told me."

"What's that?"

"You said that Vanessa staked Don."

"Right."

"But I thought the whole thing was that you had to kill Don in order for you turn back into a human?"

I smile slyly.

"You're very smart Robert."

He shakes his head. "So you're stuck being a vampire for life?"

"I don't think stuck is the word I would use."

Robert looks amazed.

"But how are you out in the sun?"

"Really strong sun block."

"What about drinking blood?"

"I'm alright for now, thanks to Don's blood. I don't know when the thirst will come back again. Maybe I'll break into an animal shelter or something."

Robert shakes his head in disbelief.

"I have to tell you something Anthony. I think I'm going to propose to Heather."

"Wow, that's big time. I think you should though."

"I had plenty of time in the hospital to think about it."

"Sometimes nearly dying is just what it takes to make you realize what's important to you."

"Yeah, so what are you going to do?"

"Well, I've been thinking. Maybe I can use my powers to help fight crime or something."

"You mean like a super vampire hero?"

"There is a lot of crime, and the police can't do everything."

"I guess you can do whatever you want now."

"Well the first thing I'm going to do is take a little flight."

"You're going to California aren't you?"

"I mean I've always wanted to see Hollywood."

"Man, how can you afford a plane ticket?"

I stretch my arms out and snap my knuckles.

"I didn't say anything about buying a plane ticket."

23

I can do this, I tell myself as I stand on the sidewalk in front of my house.

Flying is a strength that all vampires have. It's in every vampire book and novel.

Please, just allow me this one thing. I won't ever complain about being a vampire if you just give me this one power.

I don't really know who I'm talking too, some higher power in charge of vampires I suppose.

My mind is focused, concentrating hard. I try jumping in place. All that seems to happen is me doing jumping jacks.

Fly, damnit, fly!

"Anthony", I hear a voice say. "Are you trying to fly?"

"Mr. Ryan? What are you doing here?"

He is standing next to me on the sidewalk, wearing the normal suit that he always has at his office. I have no idea where he came from.

"I came to see you. You missed our session today."

"Oh wow, I'm sorry. I totally forgot."

"It's alright. I normally don't make house calls but I wanted to see how you were doing."

I smile in a way that I can never remember smiling like before.

"I think I found the motivation to no longer to be an underachiever."

"That's wonderful."

"It will be", I say."

"What are your doing about the thirst?"

I turn towards him and raise my eyes suspiciously. Does he know?

"What do you mean?" I ask slowly.

"The blood. How are you coping without it?"

"Why would I care about blood?"

He looks me in the eyes.

"You are a vampire, aren't you?"

I back up a few steps.

"How do you know?'

"I know all about this town's tainted history. And then I saw you wearing the sun block when you came to see me. I guess I put it all together."

I sigh in relief.

"I thought about telling you that day, I just didn't know how you would react. I don't know how anybody would react."

"It's alright. I understand."

"It's funny."

"What?"

"I guess maybe this is what fate and destiny had planned for me all along."

He smiles. "And now you're going to fly away?"

"I have to see about a girl."

He reaches up and begins to loosen his tie.

"I think maybe you should stay in Dale Bridge." He exclaimed.

"Why?"

He takes the tie off and than unbuttons the collar of his dress shirt.

"This town needs protection, Anthony. It needs a hero. It doesn't know it yet, but there is a villain here. And that villain is about to terrorize this town without a shed of remorse. "

"What are you talking about. What villain?"

Mr. Ryan gives a thick smile.

"Me."

"What?"

"Oh, that's right, you don't know. You see, I'm the vampire who bit Don Cramers."

I gulp. This is not a revelation I want to hear.

"He was my son."

It keeps getting worse.

"I'll be seeing you soon."

Mr. Ryan shoots me an evil smile and than looks up towards the sky.

In a quick instant, he takes off.

I look straight ahead, and then up in the air.

He's up there, flying against the wind.

I gulp again, heavily.

I'm going to need a bigger stake.

The End

Made in the USA
Charleston, SC
28 April 2013